A DANGEROUS DISGUISE

With a groan he tightened his arms and covered her mouth with his own, seeking to find the secret of her heart. Her lips were sweet against his, as sweet as in the other kisses they had shared, and for a moment the dreadful surroundings vanished, leaving only the two of them.

"Ola," he murmured, "Ola – "

For a moment she succumbed to the magic that was still there in his kiss, even now. In his arms she could forget everything.

But only briefly.

The next moment he said the words that broke the spell.

"Tell me the truth," he begged. "Tell me, Ola – "

She began to struggle against him.

"No," she said fiercely. "Let me go. It's over. Don't you know that?"

The Barbara Cartland Pink Collection

Titles in this series

A DANGEROUS DISGUISE

BARBARA CARTLAND

Barbaracartland.com Ltd

Printed and bound in Great Britain by CLE Print Ltd. of
St Ives, Cambridgeshire.

THE BARBARA CARTLAND PINK COLLECTION

Barbara Cartland was the most prolific bestselling author in the history of the world. She was frequently in the Guinness Book of Records for writing more books in a year than any other living author. In fact her most amazing literary feat was when her publishers asked for more Barbara Cartland romances, she doubled her output from 10 books a year to over 20 books a year, when she was 77.

She went on writing continuously at this rate for 20 years and wrote her last book at the age of 97, thus completing 400 books between the ages of 77 and 97.

Her publishers finally could not keep up with this phenomenal output, so at her death she left 160 unpublished manuscripts, something again that no other author has ever achieved.

Now the exciting news is that these 160 original unpublished Barbara Cartland books are ready for publication and they will be published by Barbaracartland.com exclusively on the internet, as the web is the best possible way to reach so many Barbara Cartland readers around the world.

The 160 books will be published monthly and will be numbered in sequence.

The series is called the Pink Collection as a tribute to Barbara Cartland whose favourite colour was pink and it became very much her trademark over the years.

The Barbara Cartland Pink Collection is published only on the internet. Log on to www.barbaracartland.com to find out how you can purchase the books monthly as they are published, and take out a subscription that will ensure that all subsequent editions are delivered to you by mail order to your home.

If you do not have access to a computer you can write for information about the Pink Collection to the following address :

Barbara Cartland.com Ltd.
240 High Road,
Harrow Weald,
Harrow HA3 7BB
United Kingdom.
Telephone & fax: +44 (0)20 8863 2520

THE LATE DAME BARBARA CARTLAND

Barbara Cartland who sadly died in May 2000 at the age of nearly 99 was the world's most famous romantic novelist who wrote 723 books in her lifetime with worldwide sales of over 1 billion copies and her books were translated into 36 different languages.

As well as romantic novels, she wrote historical biographies, 6 autobiographies, theatrical plays, books of advice on life, love, vitamins and cookery. She also found time to be a political speaker and television and radio personality.

She wrote her first book at the age of 21 and this was called Jigsaw. It became an immediate bestseller and sold 100,000 copies in hardback and was translated into 6 different languages. She wrote continuously throughout her life, writing bestsellers for an astonishing 76 years. Her books have always been immensely popular in the United States, where in 1976 her current books were at numbers 1 & 2 in the B. Dalton bestsellers list, a feat never achieved before or since by any author.

Barbara Cartland became a legend in her own lifetime and will be best remembered for her wonderful romantic novels, so loved by her millions of readers throughout the world.

Her books will always be treasured for their moral message, her pure and innocent heroines, her good looking and dashing heroes and above all her belief that the power of love is more important than anything else in everyone's life.

"Love can strike at any time in a blinding flash – it is so powerful that no-one can fight it."

Barbara Cartland

CHAPTER ONE
1887

The clan Chief was dead.

Colonel Owen McNewton who had been like a father to his people, had ruled them sternly but kindly for thirty years, and now he was gone.

When the burial service was over, they streamed out of the church and began the short walk to the imposing mansion where he had lived with his daughter, Ola.

The road lay slightly uphill, so that everyone could see the great building against the background of rugged Scottish scenery, at its best now that the month was June and the weather was glorious.

Ola, who was the chief mourner, forced herself not to cry as they walked away from her father, with whom she had spent the last five years after her mother's death.

She was a tall, rather stark figure as she led the procession home. Her auburn hair would have been fascinating if it had not been severely hidden away beneath a puritanical bonnet.

Her face contained many contradictions. She was beautiful, with large green eyes and a wide, generous mouth, but just now austerity had settled over her features, as though all thought of beauty was forbidden on this sad day.

Behind her walked the next clan Chief, Jonas McNewton, with his wife and numerous children. Although Ola was heiress to her father's considerable fortune, which meant only his money, but not the house and land, as they descended directly to the next Chief.

Soon she must leave Ben Torrach, this wild, beautiful place in the north of Scotland that had always been her home, and find her own niche in the world. Although the new Chief was polite, she knew he was awaiting the announcement of her departure.

The funeral feast was prepared, as lavish as tradition demanded. Owen McNewton was entertaining his friends for the last time. Ola was the perfect hostess, and everybody said that the fine old man had been given a fitting send-off.

Only one person seemed displeased. Ola saw Jonas regarding the feast with frugal disdain.

"I would not, myself, have gone to quite such expense," he sniffed.

"My father believed in treating his neighbours generously," Ola said crossly, and removed herself before he could pursue the subject.

Generous did not seem to be a word known to Jonas. The servants knew it, and were regarding him with dismay. None of them wanted to work for him.

Ola's maid, Greta, was particularly fierce.

"Work for that long streak of sour milk, after your mother and father? I should say not!"

Greta came from the little German dukedom of Saxe-Coburg-Gotha and had been maid to Ola's mother, Helene, also from the same place. On his one and only visit abroad, the young Owen had fallen in love with Helene, married her and taken her back to Scotland. The loyal Greta had come too.

She had once worked in great houses, for aristocratic masters, even once for minor royalty. But she had left glittering society behind to follow her dear mistress to 'that savage place' as she always referred to Scotland.

After Helene's death, two years ago, she had stayed on as a companion to Ola. She was thin, flat chested and grim faced, but behind the dragon exterior was the kindest heart in the world.

"When you leave this house," she had told Ola, "you must take me with you, because if I stay here I'll shoot that man."

Greta never minced words.

"But of course you'll come with me," Ola said. "I couldn't do without you. I just wish I knew where I was going."

She sighed wistfully. "If Papa hadn't become ill, we would have been on our way to London about now, to see Queen Victoria's Golden Jubilee celebrations."

How they had planned and schemed for that visit! Living in the highlands Ola had seen nothing of society, and had almost no excitement in her life. But Papa had promised her that they would stay at least two weeks in town, and enjoy all the parades and processions.

How sad he had been to disappoint her when his last illness had overtaken him. But he had insisted that he would recover in time for at least some of the festivities.

He had even refused to cancel their hotel reservation, fearful of losing the suite of rooms that he had booked, since London was fast filling up with visitors from all over the world.

"Keep the reservation open, my dear," he had told Ola. "And we will be there."

But it was not to be.

On his deathbed, he had said to her,

3

"My darling, I want you to go to London, as we planned."

"Oh no, Papa! How could I think of enjoying myself?"

"But it's what I want. You've had so little fun shut away up here. You're twenty-four. You should have gone into society years ago, but circumstances conspired against it.

"We meant to take you to London to make your debut, but then your mother became ill. Her death finished my own life. I could never rouse myself from my grief to make the effort until this year. And then it was too late. I regret my selfishness now."

"Please Papa, it doesn't matter."

"But it does. You have your life to live, and it isn't too late. You're beautiful, and you'll have money. Go and enjoy yourself, as we planned. Do all the things we meant to do together, and remember me."

She had wept but he demanded her promise, finally saying,

"Obey me, daughter!"

It was the first time her kindly father had demanded unquestioning obedience, and she could not refuse.

But now that the time had come, how could she do such a thing while she was in mourning?

Greta knew about the promise her father had exacted. Now Ola said to her,

"Do you think I could really do that?"

"The Chief was a wise man, and he knew what was good for you. Of course you must go."

At first Ola put off making her decision, but Jonas had already moved his family into her home and she was beginning to feel squeezed out.

The newspapers were full of reports of the Jubilee as the excitement mounted. It seemed incredible that one little woman had reigned over England for fifty years.

She had ascended the throne as a young girl in 1837, when she was only eighteen years old, and within three years had married Prince Albert from Saxe-Coburg-Gotha. It had always caused Ola's Mother great pleasure to think that the royal consort was a kinsman from her own little country.

The Queen had borne nine children, gone into seclusion when her husband died in 1861 and emerged only with reluctance ten years later.

During her reign her Empire had expanded over most of the globe. She was not only Queen of Great Britain, but Empress of India.

Now it seemed as though the entire world was converging on London to pay tribute to her. And Ola longed to be there, just as her loving father had understood. That was why he had insisted.

A secret excitement was growing in Ola. If only she dared!

Suddenly she jumped up and went to the window. She was looking at a view she had seen a thousand times, and which never really changed.

"I'm getting older. At twenty-four I'm practically an old maid, and I have really done very little in my life," she said.

Now the sun was shining brightly. As she looked up into the sky she felt that it was telling her to be brave and adventurous. To make a jump which would lead her into a world which she had never known before.

A world she had read about and perhaps at times even dreamt about, but which she had never thought for a moment would be hers.

She would have turned away from the window but the

sunshine held her there. She felt as if she could see her future life as more brilliant, more glamorous and more exciting than it had ever been before.

It was as if the sun itself and the clear blue sky were waiting for her answer.

Then as if it was impossible for her to say 'no', she said aloud,

"I will do it! And please help me, because I've never done anything noteworthy in my life and now I must succeed."

For a moment she stood very still, as if she was waiting for an answer.

Then, strangely enough, she heard the flutter of wings, and two white doves flew from the roof past her window and into the trees in the garden.

They were so white and, somehow, glittering in the sunshine, that she felt they were a direct message from the angels, and perhaps her father, that she should not be afraid, but do what she had promised him without any fear.

'I will do it! I will do it!' Ola told herself.

She summoned Greta to her at once.

"We're going to London," she said. "Pack my finest things. I'm going to do everything in tremendous style, just as Papa would have wanted. And if people are shocked at my doing this when I'm in mourning, well, I'll – I'll be somebody else. Nobody knows me in London."

"Well done!" said Greta at once. "You'll need a lot of new clothes."

"I'll buy them in London."

Greta gave a pleased sigh.

"I've looked forward to dressing you as you deserve to be dressed. You have beauty, if it's brought out properly, and by the time I've finished, you'll look like a Princess."

Ola stared at her.

"Greta, that's it! I'm going to be a Princess."

"How will you manage that?"

"I shall say I'm a Princess, and nobody will know any different. You can tell me all I need to know."

"I? How can I – ?"

"You lived at a court once."

"For a few months, more than twenty years ago – "

"But it doesn't change, surely? You've always told me that royal life is fixed in aspic. Everything is done in the traditional way, at the traditional time. In any case, I shan't be living at court."

"But – "

It was useless for her to protest. Ola was becoming really carried away.

"I am Her Royal Highness, Princes Relola of Oltenitza," she declared grandly.

"And where exactly is Oltenitza?" asked Greta.

Ola shrugged airily.

"I don't know. I'll decide that later."

This was so unlike the sensible young woman Greta knew that she became a little alarmed.

"Perhaps you should come down to earth," she said.

"Greta, I don't want to come down to earth. I've had my feet on the ground all my life. Now I want to soar up and up, until I fly close to the sun."

"And suppose your wings melt and you fall?"

"I don't care. I'll have the memories forever."

"All right, my dear," said Greta fondly. "You can be Princess Relola, and I'll be your lady-in-waiting." She gave a deep curtsey. "Your Royal Highness."

Ola regarded her haughtily.

"You may rise," she said.

Then she burst into a giggle of delight.

"Oh Greta," she said, "this is going to be such fun."

*

They departed next morning, leaving early because of the length of the journey. As Ben Torrach was far out in the country there was a twenty mile trip in the carriage to the nearest tiny railway station, where they caught the train for Edinburgh.

There they caught another train for the long journey south to London. They had two first class sleeping compartments, and they sat up late while Greta did Ola's hair in curlers. Greta was racking her brains to remember what she had learned when she worked for Their Royal Highnesses the Duke and Duchess of Baynich many years ago.

"They were very minor royalty," she told Ola, "but that didn't make them any less grand. On the contrary, the less important they were, the more they looked down their noses.

"The Prince of Wales came to visit them once, and he was really nice, actually winked at me. You wouldn't catch the Duke winking, or even noticing I existed."

"I don't want to be unkind to people," Ola said.

"If you're royal you don't worry what anyone thinks of you," Greta explained. "If I'm your lady-in-waiting you'll have to learn to look through me as if I were less than nothing."

"Will I?" Ola asked, startled.

"Yes. And don't call me Greta, it isn't regal."

"You should have a title too," said Ola, eager to share both the glory and the fun.

"True," Greta agreed. "Only the very highest

aristocrats are allowed to be in attendance on a royal person. I shall be Lady Krasler. But where is Oltenitza? If anyone should ask, we'd better tell the same story."

"I've decided that it's one of the little Balkan states. There are so many of them that nobody will be quite sure whether it exists or not."

"They will eventually," Greta pointed out, amused.

"Ah, but then it'll be too late. I'll have gone on to my next adventure."

"How did you think of the name?"

"Inspiration!" Ola said ecstatically. "It just came to me."

"Suppose someone asks you to say something in Oltenitzan?"

"Aristocratic Oltenitzans speak German, just like aristocratic Russians speak French," said Ola triumphantly. "Thank goodness you and Mama managed to teach it to me."

"You seem to have thought of everything."

"No, I haven't thought of anything at all. I'm making it up as I go along. That's the fun."

"And when something goes really wrong?"

"Nonsense," said Ola blithely. "How can anything go wrong?"

*

It was Ola's first experience of sleeping on a train, and it was like being rocked to sleep in a cradle. She awoke feeling refreshed, and sat looking out of the window at the English countryside rushing by, until they reached Euston Station, where trains from the north arrived in London.

To someone used to living in the country the huge station, with its vast stone arch, was a shock.

"I didn't know there were so many people in the world," Ola confided. "What do we do now?"

"We find a porter, and the porter gets us a cab."

Greta's air of lofty authority was impressive, and soon she had a porter scurrying to do her bidding.

"The Hotel Imperial, Piccadilly," she told the cab driver.

All the sights and sounds of London seemed to converge on Ola as they travelled through the streets. So much noise, bustle and colour, and here she was, in the middle of it.

The Hotel Imperial was the most imposing building Ola had ever seen, even bigger than the great house at home.

The first thing she saw as she entered was a huge copy of the official Jubilee photograph. It was a three-quarters view of Queen Victoria, sitting, looking into space with gentle melancholy. She had ruled the Empire for half a century and her eyes were full of knowledge.

On her head she wore a bonnet, whose wide lace strings tied under her chin and streamed down her breast. Beneath that bonnet the face was round and plump, with a small mouth. It might have been insipid but for a large, sharp nose that added shrewdness and character to the whole.

Both women stood for several moments looking at that tiny lady who dominated her age, and made strong men tremble.

"So that's her," Greta murmured.

"Yes, that's her," Ola said.

She began to look up in awe at the marble pillars and lofty ceilings, until Greta muttered in German,

"Don't do that. Remember you live in a palace, and this is nothing by comparison."

"Yes," Ola said hastily, in the same language.

"Perhaps it would please Your Royal Highness to sit here on this sofa while I deal with the man at the desk."

Ola had to smother a laugh at the sight of Greta advancing on the desk as though she had a bad smell under her nose. She presented the letter from the hotel confirming the reservation, and explained that the names 'Mr. McNewton and Miss McNewton' were a cover. Her Royal Highness was travelling incognito.

After that all was bustle and deference. The manager personally escorted the 'Princess' up to her suite, followed by a stream of porters carrying her bags.

Once there, her 'lady-in-waiting' inspected the suite minutely before pronouncing it just about tolerable for her royal mistress. Ola, who had never been anywhere so luxurious in her life, struggled to keep a straight face.

When the bags were finally in place, the manager bowed himself out and the door closed behind him. At once the two women collapsed with mirth, hugging each other, rocking back and forth.

The adventure had begun.

*

Ola slept peacefully all through the night, and when she woke the sun was coming in through the sides of the curtains.

She drew them back and saw that the hotel overlooked a park. Already there were people moving about under the trees. Men were trotting past on extremely fine horses.

The previous evening she and Greta had dined in the suite and gone to bed early, to sleep off the long journey. Now she felt fresh and ready for anything.

Greta bustled in to help her dress, and send a message downstairs that they required breakfast.

"What do you wish to do today?" she asked. "Visit the shops? Travel on the underground railway?"

"Greta, do people really go through a tunnel under the earth?" Ola asked.

"Of course. It's been happening for over twenty years. It's no novelty any more."

"It is if you come from Ben Torrach," Ola said with a chuckle. "I'm longing to see it, but not today. On my first day in London it is appropriate to pay my respects to Queen Victoria.

"Ola, please be serious."

"I am serious."

"You cannot just walk into Buckingham Palace."

"I am royalty offering my congratulations, and a suitable gift, to a great Queen on the occasion of her Golden Jubilee. Nothing could be more proper."

"What gift?"

"That exquisite French vase that I packed just before we left."

"You can't do it," insisted Greta, half shocked, half amused.

"Greta, I will wager you a new hat that I get into the Palace and out again without anyone discovering the truth."

"Splendid," said Greta with spirit. "I need a new hat."

Ola threw her an impish look. "Now what shall I wear?"

Still grumbling, Greta took out one of Ola's smartest walking gowns, with a matching hat. Ola had never worn them before, because they had seemed too sophisticated for the wilds of Scotland. Now she was in the right place for such clothes.

Just before she left she took a plain card from her bag and wrote on it:

'To Her Majesty Queen Victoria, with respect and admiration.

From Princess Relola of Oltenitza.'

Underneath she added the date: June 13th, 1887.

Downstairs Greta led the way out to a cab and gave the driver the address, Buckingham Palace. Deeply impressed he touched his hat and held the door open for the two great ladies.

The carriage did not take long to reach Buckingham Palace.

It was stopped at the gates. A man in uniform opened the door to ask,

"May I enquire, madam, for what reason you are coming here at this moment?"

It was Greta who replied.

"This is Her Royal Highness, Princess Relola of Oltenitza," she told him, "bringing greetings and a gift to Her Majesty on this important occasion."

The officer saluted, shut the door and said to the driver,

"Pass on."

The carriage drove to the back of the building.

Ola saw there was a door with two sentries on either side of it. As the cab drew up another man came forward, opened the door and she stepped out. Then, followed by Greta, she walked inside.

There she saw a dark suited man, standing beside a table on which there were a number of parcels which had been handed in. She walked imperiously towards him and spoke, taking care to assume an accent like Greta's so that he should not suspect that she was English.

"Princess Relola of Oltenitza. My gift is not only from myself but from all my countrymen, who wish Her Majesty well on this great occasion."

The man bowed, and ceremoniously received the parcel from her.

She had done it. She had managed to get into the Palace, and had now only to leave to have secured a triumph.

But a little imp of daring, suppressed too long, prodded her to say,

"I have come a very long way from a distant country. I wonder if I might see some part of the Palace before I go."

He looked surprised. But then another man appeared through a door and he said,

"A moment please, Your Royal Highness."

He hastened to the newcomer and spoke in a fierce whisper. Ola could just hear odd words.

" – Palace – Princess Relola – what am I to do, Your Grace?"

The man he had called 'Your Grace' then said, "I will see to it."

He walked towards Ola and she had time to see that he was about thirty years old, and very good looking.

"Good morning," he said, with a respectful bow. "I understand that Your Royal Highness has brought a present for the Queen. Her Majesty will be most grateful to you."

"Do you think she would allow me to see a little of her Palace?" Ola asked with a smile. "I've come all the way from the Balkans, and my people will want to know how your Palace compares with ours."

"I will show you what I can," the man promised. "But it's really the job of your Embassy to arrange anything like this."

Ola gave a cry.

"Hush! Hush!" she exclaimed. "I don't want them to know I am here."

He raised his eyebrows.

"But why not?"

"Because if they find out," she explained, "They will insist on my undertaking a lot of duties, meeting people I don't want to meet, most of them from the Balkans. In which

14

case I might as well have stayed where I was. I've come to see London, and while I'm here I want to meet only Londoners."

He laughed. He had an engaging twinkle in his eyes.

"I can see your point," he said. "Very well, I'll show you what I can of the Palace but you must be careful not to tell your friends, otherwise I'll be overwhelmed with people asking the same thing."

"Oh, that is so kind of you!" Ola exclaimed.

"Come along. I'm breaking all the rules on your behalf but never mind."

As they moved in the direction of the stairs Greta began to move with them, but Ola turned and said coolly,

"Lady Krasler, you have our permission to remain here."

"It might be more suitable if I – "

"Here, if you please."

"Don't worry," her escort said to Greta. "I'll take great care of her."

Greta flung her a look of indignation, but Ola refused to see it. She was determined to do this on her own.

He was, after all, an extremely good looking young man.

She took his arm and they began to mount a flight of broad stairs.

"I've not introduced myself yet," he said. "I'm the Duke of Camborne. I'm on duty here to attend to the visitors and, incidentally, to make sure that they don't take away any souvenirs."

"You can be certain they'll try," Ola replied. "After all, it's something they'll want to remember, and what could be better than one of the paintings or even a smaller object."

"I believe all the small objects have been moved out of

15

reach," said the Duke, "and I suspect some of the pictures are firmly hammered into place."

"I am curious," Ola said, "to see if this Palace, of which I have heard so much, is as marvellous as people say."

"I only hope you won't be disappointed."

They had reached the top of the stairs by now. He took her into a room where the walls were hung with paintings, and told her the names of the artists – Rembrandt, Vermeer, Holbein.

Ola's head began to spin. So many masterpieces, all in one place and all owned by the Queen.

After a while the Duke asked,

"Have you really come all the way from the Balkans just to be here for Her Majesty's Golden Jubilee? Surely you have not travelled alone?"

"Alone apart from my lady-in-waiting, whom you saw downstairs. For once I wanted to be free to spend my time as I pleased, without having to think of etiquette every moment. And it's nice to be able to forget all the worries, as well."

"What worries does Oltenitza have?"

"The Russians. Everyone knows that they are trying to gobble up the whole of the Balkan principalities one by one. Only those to whom Her Majesty has been kind enough to give her protection, feel safe."

"Her Majesty has done her best," said the Duke. "She has already arranged a number of marriages. In fact they call her the 'Matchmaker of Europe.'"

"You must be very, very proud of her. I can assure you we in Oltenitza admire her greatly."

By this time they had moved into the Throne Room.

"Is this where the debutantes are presented?" Ola asked.

"That's right. And also high ranking foreign ladies. The seats on either side of the room are filled with the relations of the ambassadors of the various countries.

"The young women themselves wait in a sitting-room until their names are called. Then they are led in by whoever is presenting them."

"It all sounds so exciting," Ola said, "and I would love to be presented myself."

"Of course you must be," the Duke replied. "I am sure Her Majesty would be delighted to invite you to Windsor Castle when all this excitement is over, if you remain in England for long."

"I will remain in England as long as I can," Ola told him. "I want to see your country as it is normally, and not just when it's celebrating a special occasion."

"I am afraid you might be disappointed with London and find it like every other capital city," the Duke said. Then he smiled. "All the same I would like to show you London at night. Perhaps you will dine with me."

Her heart beat with excitement. This was taking her gamble further than she had ever dreamed. Did she dare? Or was the risk too great?

"I would be delighted – " she said quickly.

"Would tonight be too soon? Or have you some other engagement?" enquired the Duke.

"Tonight would be very pleasant. But can you change your plans so close to the festivities? I'm sure you're very busy."

"Yes, Your Royal Highness, I am very busy, but I can assure you that when I want something I invariably get it, because I'm so determined. Now, I'm determined to give you dinner and for you to tell me more about yourself."

A little tremor went through her. Talking about herself would be dangerous, she knew.

But then her head went up. What was an adventure without risk?

"I shall be happy to do so," she said.

CHAPTER TWO

As they continued walking through the Palace the Duke said,

"I want to know how you are brave enough to come here almost alone, with only one lady-in-waiting to keep you safe."

"But I'm quite safe," Ola said, laughing. "I can look after myself. In Oltenitza the ladies are taught to be very strong. We ride hard and learn to shoot."

The shooting was true for Ola. Papa had taught her, and praised her straight aim.

"You can shoot?" he asked, amused.

"Why do you laugh? I'm an excellent shot. I can hit a bull's eye at fifty paces – at least – that is – no, take no notice of me."

"Why not? I'm interested in a lady who can shoot so well."

But Ola had recollected that gentlemen scorned ladies who were good at masculine pursuits, and the last thing that a clever woman did was to announce the fact.

"But I cannot shoot at all," she laughed. "I was just boasting. Tell me some more about London, you must know it very well."

"I can hardly call myself a Londoner," the Duke said.

"But I'll try to make sure you enjoy England and not just London."

"I would love to see more of England."

"Tonight I'll take you to a quiet place for dinner, where we can escape the festivities for a while. In my opinion they can sometimes be overdone, and last too long."

"That's exactly what I feel about anything which is royal," Ola agreed. "Every ceremony is dragged out until you feel you want to run away, and be alone."

"I should think someone as beautiful as you must find it hard to be alone," the Duke said.

Ola laughed.

"Thank you for the compliment, but I like my own company. Then I can dream of all the marvellous things I might do if I were free."

"What would the marvellous things be?" he enquired, smiling.

"I will make a list and tell you tonight," Ola said.

As they walked downstairs at the end of the tour the Duke said,

"I am sorry but I must leave you now. I have to be on duty at a grand luncheon Her Majesty is giving for overseas visitors. Of course, you should really be one of them."

"No! No!" Ola exclaimed. "I have to go to too many of that sort of function."

"But are you quite certain I shouldn't contact your ambassador?"

"I should very much dislike it if you did that," Ola replied with perfect truth. "He'll want to move me into the Embassy."

"Very well, I'll respect your wishes. But do you mean that you don't intend to meet Her Majesty at all? Is there nothing that you wish to say to her?"

"Nothing except my greetings that I have already delivered with my gift," said Ola. "I should like to see her, of course, but only from a distance – perhaps when she is out riding in her carriage. If you can tell me when she means to do that, I shall be glad."

"Very well, if I hear news of such an event, I will let you know. But I must warn you that this happens very rarely. Her Majesty lives mostly in seclusion, and it is rare for her to be as accessible as she has become during the Jubilee celebrations. She likes to spend more time at Frogmore just now."

"Frogmore?"

"It's near Windsor. Her husband, the late Prince Albert was buried there, and although he has been dead for over twenty-five years she feels his loss particularly at this time.

"She should have celebrated her Jubilee with him at her side, and it breaks her heart that she cannot. So she stays at Frogmore and then takes the train to London, and travels by carriage to Buckingham Palace."

"But is it an open carriage, so that she can be seen?" Ola asked eagerly.

"Sometimes. It depends if she is tired. And of course she will travel in an open carriage to Westminster Abbey for the service of thanksgiving."

"Thank you. Somehow I shall contrive to see her. I must."

"If it's so important, let me take you to her."

"No," she said quickly. "It must be from a distance. I can't explain. I have a reason but – I can't tell you what it is."

"Very well, as you wish. Now, about tonight. At which hotel are you staying?"

"The Imperial."

"One of the best hotels in London. I'll be there at a

quarter to eight."

"I'll be waiting for you," she told him, "and I'm known for being very punctual."

As they reached the bottom of the stairs, the Duke said suddenly,

"You must promise me not to vanish."

"Why should I vanish?"

"Because you are so unique. I'm afraid that, just as you appeared unexpectedly, so you'll vanish and I'll think I've been dreaming."

"I promise you not to vanish – until after tonight."

Ola held out her hand and he took it in both of his.

"It has been a great joy to meet you," he told her. "I'll be counting the hours until I see you again."

"And so will I," she said, meaning it.

As 'Lady Krasler' rose to her feet in readiness, the Duke murmured,

"Will your dragon feel it necessary to accompany you tonight?"

"I'm sure she will," said Ola. "But I shall not feel it at all necessary."

"Just the two of us then?"

"Just the two of us," she said, aware that her heart was beating a little faster at the thought.

As she drove off, the Duke bowed to her from the steps of the Palace and she waved her hand to him.

"Oh, that was the most exciting thing that ever happened to me," she said ecstatically.

"Hmm!" said Greta, regarding her with suspicion.

"Oh, Greta don't be cross with me. It was such fun. And tonight he's taking me to dinner." Seeing rebellion in her companion's eye she said quickly, "just the two of us."

"Shame on you. You've barely met him."

"Listen, we have a lot of work to do," Ola said, not answering her directly. "First, we have to buy you a new hat."

"But you won the bet."

"Yes, but I'm going to buy a lot of new clothes this afternoon, so you must have something too."

"You've got lots of clothes."

"But I've realised that they're all hopelessly out of fashion. None of my dresses have bustles."

"Bustles are out of fashion."

"But they came back, and now they're simply enormous. Haven't you seen the women at the hotel, and walking along the streets? They make me feel so dowdy."

Greta was forced to concede the point.

"But how can we obtain fashionable clothes at a moment's notice?" she objected. "It takes several days for a dressmaker to complete a garment. I shall seek advice at the hotel."

Luck was with them. At the reception desk they found an extremely genteel lady who informed them that for those who needed fashionable attire quickly a visit to Regent Street was the only answer.

Arriving in Regent Street was like arriving in heaven. Dress shops, hat shops, glove shops. Shops that sold items of 'delicacy'. They visited one of these first, and purchased white silk petticoats, and several pairs of drawers that came below Ola's knees and were trimmed with the prettiest lace and coloured ribbon.

Corsets too were daintily trimmed, and tightened her waist almost to nothing. Finally there was the bustle, a light wire mesh cage which was fixed around the waist with strings and protruded at the back, so that the skirt was draped over it.

There were shoes to be bought, and hats. As she had

promised, Ola purchased a hat for Greta, who was so delighted that she ceased predicting dire consequences if Ola dined alone with a man.

As last there was the evening gown. It came down to a choice between a brilliant creation in deep blue silk gauze, or a frothy confection in gold satin. Ola insisted on buying the latter, from an instinctive feeling that the Duke would like gold.

She caught Greta regarding her suspiciously, almost as though she could read her thoughts. To distract her, Ola purchased two dresses for Greta as well, explaining that her chief lady-in-waiting must be well dressed.

"So I've been promoted to *chief* lady-in-waiting, have I?" asked Greta. She tried to sound grim, but the two silk garments had pleased her.

They returned to the hotel in triumph. Ola spent the next three hours taking a nap before rising to take a refreshing bath. Greta had arranged for a light meal that she insisted Ola should eat.

"But I'm going to have dinner," Ola protested.

"You'll have something first," Greta said, adding darkly, "he may ply you with strong drink."

She had been heating the curling tongs, and as soon as Ola was dressed she got to work, arranging her auburn hair in an elaborate style.

They spent some time considering jewellery, and finally decided on a ruby and gold necklace that Ola's mother had brought with her from Coburg. It had a slightly exotic, un-English appearance that she felt would help her 'Balkan' pose. Matching ear-rings and bracelet completed the effect.

When everything was finished she stood and looked at herself in the long mirror, and could hardly believe that this was herself.

This woman was beautiful. She was assured, imperious, magnificent. She was a Princess.

As she thought of her forthcoming meeting with the Duke, she could not help feeling a thrill go through her.

'It's because I'm so excited at seeing England,' she told herself.

At the same time she knew that the Duke was, without exception, the most charming and handsome man she had ever met, and the thought of spending an evening alone with him made her eyes shine.

At last a message arrived to say that His Grace, the Duke of Camborne was downstairs.

Because she did not want to seem too eager, she kept him waiting for almost ten minutes before she descended the stairs, accompanied by a grim-faced Greta.

She saw him before he saw her, and had a few moments to contemplate him. He was sitting next to an elderly lady, engaging her in conversation. Now and then he smiled, and Ola drew in her breath at how handsome he was, and how his smile seemed to fill the room.

Then he saw her and instantly rose to his feet. He was splendid in evening attire, with a black cloak over his shoulder, and a gleaming black top hat ready to be put onto his head. He smiled again, but this time it was just for her, and her heart leapt for she knew that he admired her.

He bowed low as she approached.

"Your Royal Highness," he said.

"I am sorry I was not ready," she apologised, "but I was working hard to look my best for you."

The Duke laughed.

"You are fishing for compliments," he teased. "You know you look lovely. I only hope the dinner will be worthy of you."

Ola thought that it would be difficult to think of

anything during the meal, but the man who was with her. However she knew that such thoughts were unbecoming in a young lady, so she concealed them, and merely said,

"I'm looking forward to eating English food in an English restaurant. That in itself will be a treat I have not enjoyed before."

She spoke carefully, remembering to use the Coburg accent she had learnt from her mother and Greta.

"Then come along, my carriage is waiting for you," the Duke replied. "I will be very disappointed if this is not one of the special evenings which you remember of the Royal Jubilee."

"I am sure that will happen," Ola said. She smiled at Greta, who bobbed a curtsey.

Then the Duke gave her his arm and they swept out together.

This was it, she thought. This was the moment of glory that she had promised herself when she planned this venture.

The Duke's carriage was extremely grand, with a coat of arms on the sides, and two men on the box wearing the Camborne livery.

As they travelled along Piccadilly Ola looked eagerly out of the windows at the crowds thronging the street. So many lights. So much bustle and excitement. After her dull life this was like stepping into a dream.

"It's so thrilling," she murmured.

"But surely the capital city of Oltenitza is much the same?" enquired the Duke.

She saw the pit at her feet and quickly avoided it.

"No capital is the same as London," she declared. "Everyone knows that it is the biggest, brightest city in the world. It has art, science, music, theatre. My own little capital is a village by comparison."

She hoped he would not ask what her 'little capital' was called, because for the moment her inspiration had dried up. Luckily he did not pursue the subject.

"I will admit that London is at its best just now," he agreed, "putting on its finest feathers to impress visitors. But I like it at other times too, when it's just itself. Tonight I'm not taking you to one of the big, glittering restaurants, but a small one, in a side street, where only really knowledgeable people go.

"We can be very private, unless of course you would feel nervous about that. Would it be more proper if there were many people around, watching us?"

Ola gave a merry little laugh. "But sir, it's well known that all English gentlemen are honourable. What could I have to fear?"

"I suppose even an English gentleman might get carried away by his feelings?" he said lightly.

"But what feelings? We have only just met," she teased him. "I know I have nothing to fear."

In saying this she knew she was slightly avoiding the truth. They might have only just met, but she was already in danger of being carried away by her own feelings, and very much hoped that he was too.

At last the carriage stopped in a narrow street, with poor lighting. Heads turned as the footman jumped down to open the door, bowing as she stepped down.

At first she thought the restaurant was no different to the rustic places in villages around her home, but then the Duke led her through the building and to a garden at the rear, hung with fairy lamps.

"Oh, how beautiful," Ola exclaimed.

Their table was under the trees, in view of the other diners, but sufficiently apart that she could almost feel that they were alone. As they walked together she knew that people were looking at them and thinking what a splendid couple they made.

'And we do,' she thought. 'Oh, if only this could go on forever!'

When he asked her what she liked to eat, she replied that she would leave everything to him. He spoke to the head waiter in strong, masterful accents, and ordered a bottle of the best champagne.

"To toast our meeting," he said.

Ola had never tasted champagne before, and she thought she had gone to paradise. But real paradise was the smile in his eyes as they met hers over the rim of the glass.

"Your Royal Highness," he said.

"You mustn't call me that. Someone might hear."

"What shall I call you?" he asked.

"Ola."

"Not Relola?"

"I prefer Ola from my friends. But now you must tell me your name."

"John," he said. "John Sedgewick, Duke of Camborne."

"Is that all?" she laughed. "Don't English Dukes always have lots of titles?"

"How well informed you are. Viscount Allanlee, Baron Frensham, Baron Lockton, and some others that I can't remember. And you? I'm sure you have a host of minor titles too."

"Of course, but I can never remember even one or two of mine. I think I forget them on purpose. They make me forget about who I really am inside."

"And who is that?"

She shook her head.

"I don't know. I'm still trying to discover. It may take a long time."

A sudden alert look came into his eyes.

"Do you feel like that too?" he asked.

"Oh yes. You also, it seems."

He nodded, still looking at her as though trying to discover something.

"I've always felt like that," he said. "Right from the moment I realised that I was going to be buried under all those titles, none of which seemed to have anything to do with me. I'm sure you understand that."

He meant that she understood from experience, but the fact was that she had looked into his heart and seen everything by instinct.

"When you hear them spoken it is like listening to a story about somebody else," she said. "Not you at all. You think, who is this person, and why do people look at me when they speak about her?"

"Yes, yes," he said urgently. In his eagerness he seized her hands. "That's exactly how I feel, but I never found anyone else who could follow my thoughts. It's like coming out of a dark wood into the light, and finding a sweet presence waiting for me."

A cough from over their heads brought them out of the spell that had enclosed them, making them look up hastily to see the waiter standing there with the first course.

They recollected themselves and concentrated on the food, both a little dazed by what had happened without warning.

Later Ola had to admit to herself that she could hardly remember what she had eaten.

But she could recall almost every word he had spoken.

She urged him to talk about his life, and he did so, almost as if there was safety in such personal topics.

"You don't live in London all the time, of course," she asked him.

"No, just part of the year, for the season. That's the social season which starts in May. Debutantes are presented at court, there are balls, parties, regattas on the Thames. It goes on until early August, and then everyone goes north to shoot grouse, starting on the twelfth."

"To Scotland, yes," she murmured, thinking of the many grouse shooting parties she had seen arriving.

"You know Scotland?" he asked in some surprise.

"Only by repute," she said hurriedly. "I know about the 'glorious twelfth' and the hunting, shooting and fishing. Do you enjoy 'the season'?"

He sighed ruefully.

"Not a great deal, I must admit. I like to be out in the country, riding my favourite horses, walking with my dogs."

She had often heard her father talk like that. It was enchanting to hear the same sentiments from the man who was weaving spells about her heart.

"So you don't like the formality of London?" she said. "People bowing and scraping because you're so important?"

"They only think I'm important because I have a great title," the Duke replied. "But as a man I am happier in the country because I'm alone with my animals, and they are not concerned whether I am a Duke or the pantry boy."

Ola laughed.

"That's what you say, but I'll wager they are taught to bow from the moment they come into this world," she said.

"You wouldn't say that if you could see my dogs," the Duke said, grinning. "They think they own me, rather than the other way around. I have five, four pedigree and one mongrel, and the mongrel is the loftiest of them all."

"I like that," Ola said, delighted. "I once had a dog who was just the same. I loved him so much, he was my best friend. We used to go walking together, and as he had rather a long coat all the thistles would stick to it, and it would take me an hour to get them out."

"You did that? Not a footman?"

"I couldn't have let a servant do it," she said with an air of horror. "Joey wouldn't have liked that at all. It had to be me."

"Joey? You gave your dog an English name?"

"He was a gift from an English friend," she said quickly. To get off dangerous ground she said, "You must miss your country home."

"Yes, I love the place. It's very old and has been in my family for many years. It is exactly like the houses you read about in story books and I have, although I say it, an outstanding collection of horses."

Ola gave a cry.

"I love riding," she said. "My favourite horse can jump higher than any other horse in the royal stable. I take him out every morning before breakfast."

"I will certainly show you my horses," the Duke promised.

"I would love to see them, but I suppose they are not in London."

"Most of them are in the country." A thought seemed to strike him. "Your Royal Highness – "

"Ola," she corrected him. She wanted to hear her name from his mouth.

"Ola," he said. "I must compliment you on your English accent."

"Oh no!" she disclaimed. "In Oltenitza I am held to speak English well, but in England I know that my deficiencies must be very apparent."

"Not at all. In fact, your accent has grown more

naturally English as we have talked."

He was right. She had been so absorbed in his company that she had forgotten to maintain her Coburg accent.

"Ah, but I am a great mimic," she said quickly. "My accent improves because I am talking with you."

"That must be it," he agreed.

"Go on telling me about your horses."

"I have one in London, which I ride in the Row every morning – "

"Excuse me? Row? You all ride in rows?" she asked, trying to look as puzzled as possible. She needed to show a little ignorance to put him off the scent.

"The Row is Rotten Row, in Hyde Park."

"It is rotten? Then how do you ride there?"

He laughed. "It isn't really rotten. Nearly two hundred years ago we had a king called William III, who used it as a short cut to get to Kensington Palace. So it became known as 'the king's road', which, in French, is 'route de roi'.

"And as no Englishman has ever been able to speak French without mangling it, it became corrupted to 'Rotten Row'."

"So, this William III – he was French?"

"No, he was Dutch."

"So why did they not name the road in Dutch?"

"Because the English are even worse at Dutch than they are at French," said the Duke grinning.

"*Gott in Himmel!*" said Ola, feeling that a touch of German would serve her well at this moment.

"Exactly!" he said, his eyes gleaming with amusement.

"You English are all *wahnsinnig*."

"I have a horrid feeling that that means stupid."

"No, no, it means crazy."

"Oh yes, crazy. I agree to that."

"I think I should leave quickly before my brain explodes."

"*No!*"

He took her hand in a firm grip.

"You must not leave," he said, and there was a strange, intense light in his eyes. "You *must* not."

Ola could not have left at that moment for anything in the world. While he held her hand in his so powerfully and looked at her with that disturbing light in his eyes, she knew herself to be helpless.

She had a wild impulse to say, 'I will do whatever you wish. You have only to command me.'

But she must fight it, remembering that she was a Princess, and he was a commoner. It was hard because everything inside her was saying that this was a man she could admire, even adore. She longed to yield to that feeling, but she dared not.

Fear made her behave imperiously, looking down at his hand grasping hers, then giving him an amazed stare.

"Forgive me," he said. "I had no right to touch you against your will."

She wanted to cry out, 'But it isn't against my will. I want to touch you back. I want to be in your arms, feeling your lips on mine. I shall always want that.'

But she only said,

"Why are you so abrupt and hasty?"

"Because it's very important that you don't leave. More important than I can say."

"Why is it so important?" she asked.

"For reasons which – which I cannot explain. Please

– stay with me. And do not be offended."

Her heart swelled with joy because she was sure she understood him. He would not let her go because he was as drawn to her as she was to him. But, of course, he could not say so.

"I am not offended," she said gently.

"And you will stay?"

She smiled.

"I have no choice, since you are still holding my hand so tightly"

He looked down at their clasped hands as though he had only just discovered them. For a long moment he did not move. He seemed possessed by the tension between them, as was she.

"If I release you," he said slowly, at last, "will you promise not to run away?"

She sighed, so softly that he could not hear.

"I promise."

Reluctantly he disengaged his hand from hers, and she felt an almost physical pain at the parting.

'What's happening to me,' she thought wildly. 'This is mad, dangerous. I should stop it now before it's too late.'

But she knew that it was already too late.

It had always been too late.

CHAPTER THREE

"Now that I've agreed to stay," she said shakily, "you must go on telling me about your horses. They sound so – so fascinating."

She could not remember a single word he had said about his horses, but it seemed a safe subject.

"Yes," he said vaguely. "My horses. I have one in London, to ride in Rotten Row. Society goes to Hyde Park, and parades there, on foot or on horseback."

"Then I must go," she said.

"I believe you would enjoy it. Of course I left the rest of my horses in the country because, as you can imagine, I really have very little time to myself."

"Don't you like anything about London at all? Not even being at court?"

They had both calmed down now, managing to slip back into normal-sounding conversation, almost as though there was nothing else humming beneath.

"In some ways being at court is the worst of all. I'm constantly in the middle of – " he checked himself.

"Go on," she encouraged.

"If I do, I'll sound like a conceited coxcomb."

"I promise not to think so."

"Very well. I am in your hands. I'm constantly in the

middle of the marriage mart. Have you any idea how difficult it is to own things that people want, and can only get by marrying you? They want your money and your title, and they will take you as well because that's the price, but you, yourself, as a person, are almost irrelevant to them."

He smiled at Ola. "But of course you know all this. It must be exactly the same for you."

"Ah yes!" she said with an air of wisdom. "Suitors. Such a trial."

"If a Duke is afflicted, a Princess must be a thousand times more so. How one longs to escape! In fact, is that the real reason you – ?"

"Ssh!" she stopped him with one finger over her lips. "Some things are best left unsaid."

"Of course. Forgive me."

"Tell me about your family," Ola enquired.

"I have two sisters who are married, both very happily, I'm glad to say. My father died five years ago when, of course, I took his place.

"Then my mother died two years ago. She was so unhappy after my father's death that she only wanted to join him in heaven. She couldn't face being alone on earth."

"How could she have felt alone when she had you?" Ola asked.

"I can't compensate her for the loss of the man she loved. A son isn't the same thing at all. I was fond of travelling, but I began to stay at home, to be with her when she needed me. But eventually she told me, very sweetly, to take myself off. She said she needed to be alone.

"I've always wondered whether that was true, or if she was just being kind to me. My mother was the kindest woman in the world. Anyway, I did a lot of travelling."

"Tell me about your travels," begged Ola.

"But I was going to ask about yours. They must be far

36

more interesting."

"Oh no, one sees so little, nothing but receptions and formal occasions." She laughed. "I must know every ballroom in Europe."

"And are admired in every ballroom in Europe," said the Duke, gallantly.

"You're too kind to say so. But after all, what is a ballroom? It's the country outside that matters, and which I never see. So I want to hear all you have to tell."

She listened, fascinated, as he talked about the places he had visited. She had never been anywhere but Scotland in her life, but this man had been all over Europe, France, Italy, Spain, and then further, to India and Egypt.

She listened entranced as he described the pyramids, the desert, the Nile. Her eyes shone as he talked about Venice and Rome.

This was what she had always wanted to know. The men she had met in the past had only talked about how they admired her, and what they felt for her. Since she did not admire them, and suspected that their real feelings were for her father's money, their conversation did not interest her.

"One day," she murmured, "I must see these things myself. I should love to go to Venice, and ride in a gondola along the Grand Canal."

"Perhaps you will travel on to Venice when you leave here?" the Duke suggested.

"Oh no," she said, with a sigh. "That wouldn't be the same – "

"The same?" he echoed.

She had meant that Venice was a place to be visited with the person you love, and that being there alone was not the same, but she had spoken without thinking. Now she checked herself, realising that she could hardly say this aloud.

"I felt very strange being in Venice by myself," he said after a moment. "The Grand Canal looked beautiful from a gondola – but I was alone."

Now she knew that he had understood the things she could not say.

"And then?" she asked. "Afterwards?"

"I came home and my uncle, who is on the Queen's staff, told me that he'd found me a place at court, and I should accept it for the honour of the family.

"Well, I had pleased myself, so I realised that I should now think of the family. Of course what they really want is for me to marry and produce a heir to the title. But I haven't met anyone with whom I want to spend the rest of my life. So, much to their annoyance, I have remained unmarried.

"One day I shall return to Venice, and take that gondola again. But this time, I shan't be alone."

Ola knew a frisson of alarm. This adventure was taking her into uncharted waters.

But at the same time there was a thrill of excitement. The sensible thing would be to pull back now, but she could not be sensible. It was like being on a galloping horse, sailing over high, dangerous fences, not knowing what was going to happen next, whether it would be triumph or disaster, but she was exhilarated beyond belief.

"Go on telling me about your life," she said.

"Shouldn't you be telling me about yourself?" he asked.

Ola shook her head.

"No, my own life seems to me completely uninteresting."

This was true in a way that he could not imagine.

"But if I talk about myself," he said, "I must also talk about you, who have come into my life so unexpectedly, and fascinated me in a way that has never happened before."

Ola laughed, a little shakily.

"Do you really expect me to believe that?"

"It happens to be the truth," he replied seriously, "and if you are surprised, then I am surprised too."

"Yes," Ola said after a moment. "I am surprised."

There was a sudden silence. They were both shaken.

Suddenly the Duke looked around him with a start. While they had been absorbed in each other, time had passed and now the restaurant was almost empty.

Ola raised her head, also startled. Where had the time gone while she was in the enchanting company of this man?

"I should have taken you somewhere where we could dance," he said. "But after your long journey you should go to bed early. Can we meet again tomorrow, and I'll show you some of the Jubilee celebrations?"

"Oh yes, I would like to do that," Ola said. "You are so kind, when you must be busy."

"I'm on duty much of the time," the Duke agreed. "But I consider it part of my duty to look after you, and not let you get into trouble."

"Do you think I'm likely to get into trouble?" she teased.

"Well, I must admit to another reason. I want to have you to myself."

Ola smiled.

"I was very lucky to meet you."

Then he said something she did not understand.

"I do hope so."

"Surely there can be no doubt of it? I know when I'm being lucky," said Ola.

She thought his manner became uneasy.

"Do any of us really know what is happening in our lives? Aren't there always unseen things that make a difference, although we don't know about them – and may never know about them."

Ola stared at him. "Why do you talk in mysteries?"

"Because they surround us all the time. Don't you ever feel that?"

"Yes," she sighed, thinking of how she was deceiving him. She was not what he believed, and there were mysteries surrounding her that he did not suspect.

"We must always be on our guard," he said, "but I'm sure you have someone in heaven looking after you."

The way he said it made her smile a little shyly before she answered,

"I only hope that's true. But I said my prayers before I came here and I think in finding you, one of them has certainly been answered."

"Then I must make sure you continue to feel like that. There are a great many different things going on over the next few days – parties, processions and fireworks."

"Oh, I love fireworks. We have them sometimes in Oltenitza and how the people love them.

There was silence for a moment. Then the Duke said,

"We hear very strange stories about the Balkans and how the Russians menace you. Is that really true?"

"I am afraid it is," Ola replied. "Only one thing makes them pause, and that is where a country is protected by the Queen of England, through a strategic marriage."

"I hate to tell you this," said the Duke, "but we all know that sooner or later she will run out of royal brides."

An imp of mischief made her say,

"Perhaps they'll give me a royal prince. Her Majesty has several sons, and grandsons."

"Would you do that?" he asked. "Enter an arranged marriage for the sake of your country?"

He did not look at her as he said this, and something told her that the question saddened him.

"We must all do our duty," she said. "But it would be very hard to marry without love. In fact, it would almost make life meaningless."

"Totally meaningless," he said firmly.

"I think we all dream of finding the perfect person," Ola said softly, "Someone who will forgive our faults and go on loving us even though we're not perfect, someone who will understand the things we do that might seem strange and – " she broke off before she was tempted to say too much.

He was looking at her curiously.

"You almost seem to speak with a particular meaning," he said. "As though the words meant something special to you."

"No, not at all," Ola disclaimed quickly. "It's only that I've seen many marriages made for ambition – are there any other kind at court? – and they were so unhappy that I resolved to find something better."

"If they will allow you."

"Yes, if they will allow me."

"Shall I tell you something?" the Duke said. "When I listen to you I seem to hear my own heart speaking. This is exactly what I've always thought. True love means loving somebody at their worst as well as their best.

"When I marry – and I must do so one day – I want a woman with a great heart. But where am I to find that in the marriage mart, where I meet only simpering girls being pushed at me by their ambitious Mamas, who want my title?"

"It is equally sad for both of us," she said.

He seemed to give himself a little shake. "Yes, but enough of sadness. Tomorrow we shall simply enjoy being together, and I shall keep you to myself. I don't want to share you with other men, who will try to intrude because you're so beautiful."

Ola laughed.

"Perhaps it's just because I'm a Princess. So if we meet anyone, just say I am a friend from overseas. You can call me Fraulein Schmidt."

"You are making it all very mysterious," the Duke replied, "but I see your point. Even so, I think I'll have to fight the other fellows to keep 'Fraulein Schmidt' to myself."

"Thank you, kind sir. And can we do all the exciting things that I'm not usually allowed to do, and which are usually the only things worth doing?"

"Anything you want, I promise. I shall send a message to your hotel tomorrow morning, to let you know the arrangements. That is – if it shall please Your Royal Highness."

"Whatever you arrange will please me," she said recklessly. "Oh, this is so much like a lovely dream, that I'm afraid I'll wake up."

"I won't let you," the Duke answered with a smile, "and that's a promise. And now I must take you home. It's much later than I thought. The dragon who protects you will be very angry with me. But I've enjoyed myself so much with you that I couldn't tear myself away. You are one of the most exciting women I've ever talked to. I never know what you are going to say next."

"That's because I've said very little," she laughed. "Men always think a woman is witty when she lets them do the talking."

He roared with laughter.

"Well done!" he said appreciatively. "That will teach me to be more cautious. But, of course, by saying that, you disprove your own argument by being genuinely witty. Now I'm really curious to know what else you will say."

She looked at him mischievously.

"I think you'd be very surprised by some of the things I could say."

"Now, what do you mean by that?"

"Nothing," she backtracked hastily, regretting the moment of madness that made her admit anything so reckless.

"That isn't true. You meant something."

"Perhaps, but I don't think I'll tell you just now," she said, assuming an imperious voice to silence him.

As they drove back to the hotel she said,

"I shall lie awake tonight, thinking of the wonderful things I'm going to do."

"If I lie awake it will be because I'm thinking of you," he replied.

There was an expression in his eyes which made her feel a little tremor go through her, and she dared not look at him.

He took her hand and raised it to his lips.

"I thought I was an honourable man," he said, "but now I find that perhaps you are not as safe with me as you thought. Your Royal Highness – Ola – I want to kiss you. I want that very much."

Her heart was beating wildly.

"Are you going to?" she whispered.

His hand tightened on hers.

"No," he said. "It's too soon. But I warn you, tomorrow I may not think that it's too soon. Perhaps you should beware."

She smiled at him in the dim light of the carriage.

"I am not afraid," she said. "Perhaps it is you who should be afraid."

"I am. I feel as though I've been caught up in

something strange and mysterious, something over which I have no control. Do you feel that way too?"

"Yes," she murmured. "Oh yes."

And then she realised that the carriage had stopped. The journey was over.

He came inside the hotel with her, as far as the foot of the stairs.

"Goodnight," he said, pressing her hand. "I do hope you sleep well."

"I doubt if I will," she said. "I have too many things to think about."

He nodded.

"Until tomorrow," he murmured.

Then he turned quickly and left her there.

Walking up the stairs, Ola felt it had all been a dream.

'How can this possibly have happened?' she asked herself. 'And what will become of me? One day, just as I've appeared unexpectedly, so I'll have to disappear. To me this is a dream come true. But to him it will be a dream soon forgotten.'

Greta was waiting up for her.

"Well?" she demanded eagerly. "What happened? Did he suspect anything?"

Ola shook her head, her eyes shining.

"You actually got away with it?" Greta breathed. "I thought he would see through you, if you had to talk for a long time."

"He talked most of the time. I just listened."

"Well, thank goodness that's over. You mustn't take such a risk again."

"I'm seeing him tomorrow," Ola said dreamily.

"What?"

"He's going to show me the sights."

"Which means that more people will meet you, and the more who hear you called a Princess, the more who may suspect something."

"No, we're pretending that I'm Fraulein Schmidt."

Greta stared.

"Are you telling me," she said in a dazed voice, "that you will be a commoner, pretending to be a Princess who is pretending to be a commoner?"

"Yes."

"You have taken leave of your senses."

"Oh yes," Ola sighed. "I've known that for the last two hours."

"My dear, you frighten me."

"Don't be frightened. I'm not. I'm not going to let myself be scared. It's no way to live."

"But how far can this go? What happens when he has to know the truth?"

"I don't know. I don't want to think about that."

"But if you're falling in l– "

Greta was silenced by Ola's hand over her mouth.

"Hush! Don't say it. I just want to enjoy this time, however short it is."

She would not say any more while Greta helped her to undress, and brushed out her hair. But deep inside she was troubled.

'How will he ever forgive me for deceiving him?' she thought.

When she thought of the Duke, there was a little sob in her heart. She was doing something wrong and she felt she should run away.

Then she told herself that nothing and no one could stop her seeing him tomorrow.

'Perhaps when tomorrow is over I will have to

disappear,' she thought. 'But not until then.'

But she did not want to leave him. She wanted to stay. She wanted this wonderful time to last as long as possible.

And she prayed that there would be no ugly, angry reckoning when it all came to an end.

*

When Ola awoke she knew that this was going to be an exciting day and wonderful things were going to happen. She got out of bed and looked at herself in the mirror to see if she looked tired and worn out. Instead she seemed younger than she actually was and her eyes were shining.

'I must make myself look lovely for him,' she thought. 'I wonder if he is thinking of me, as I am thinking of him.'

She tried to be realistic. He had so many duties. He would be thinking of them, not of her. That was only right.

It was a saddening thought.

What she longed to do was send him a note saying that he was in her heart. But a lady could not do that, even when the gentleman had seemed attracted by her, because as every woman knew – and if she did not, she soon learned – men could split their minds into different compartments, and think of only one at a time, without, apparently, noticing that it contradicted the others.

She tried to picture him sitting at his desk, studying important papers, perhaps preparing for an appointment with the Queen. And then, remembering that he had made a promise to a girl he'd met the night before.

And regretting it?

It would be terrible if he were to think her a nuisance.

Her father had always attracted much admiration from women, but he was never impressed by it.

"The more women talk the less I believe them," he had once said.

"Of course you believe them, my dear, when they are flattering you," his wife had replied, amused. She knew her husband cared only for her.

Her father had snorted, as he always did when he was embarrassed.

"They do it so clumsily," he grunted. "It's not for a woman to run after a man, but for a man to run after a woman." Catching his wife giving him a teasing look, he had added hastily, "an unmarried man, of course."

She remembered that now, and knew that it would be terrible if the Duke thought she was running after him.

'He must have a dozen women doing that already,' she told herself sadly. 'He's so handsome. He's probably forgotten me.'

For a moment her sense of humour came to her rescue.

'Of course, I'm a Princess, which gives me the advantage.'

But then she sighed and became despondent again.

'He'd probably have said the same to any Princess. That's the problem with having the advantage. You never really know what the other person is thinking.'

As she was drinking coffee there was a knock on the door, which Greta answered, returning with a letter.

"This was delivered for you downstairs," she said, handing it to Ola.

On the letter was written,

To Her Royal Highness, the Princess Relola.

Tearing it open, she read,

I shall be downstairs at 10 o'clock precisely. We are going riding.

John.

'He hasn't forgotten me,' her heart sang.

Then a terrible thought seized her.

47

"Greta, did you pack my riding habit?"

"Of course I did," said Greta, bristling with indignation at this slur.

In moments she had taken out the black broadcloth habit and was brushing it down. It fitted snugly onto Ola's trim figure, emphasising her tiny waist and flaring hips. Beneath it she wore a snowy white shirt, frilled at the neck and down the front, with a pearl brooch at her throat.

For her head there was a cheeky black hat, decorated with white streamers that flowed down her back.

At precisely ten o'clock she made her way downstairs. The Duke was waiting for her, dressed in an immaculately tailored jacket, riding breeches and gleaming black boots. As soon as he saw her, he bowed.

"Good morning, Fraulein Schmidt," he said. "Your humble escort has arrived, and he thinks you look like the sun itself. Every man who sees you with me will be jealous that I have beaten him to the winning post."

She laughed aloud with delight.

"You speak as if I were a horse," she teased.

"No, you're the prize. Now, come with me, and let me show you a marvel."

She followed him out of the hotel to where a groom was standing on the pavement, holding three horses. One was his own mount, one was a powerful black stallion, the last was a dainty little milk white mare.

Ola exclaimed with pleasure at the sight of the mare.

"She is yours?"

"No. Don't tell anyone, but I borrowed her from the royal stables. Come, let me help you mount."

With his hands on her waist, she was swiftly in the saddle.

"Now we're going to Rotten Row," he said.

Her heart soared with joy. Whatever the problems, she would worry about them later. For now there was only this perfect day, this man, this happiness.

CHAPTER FOUR

"Are we far from Hyde Park?" Ola asked as they cantered along Piccadilly.

"No, it's just at the end of this road, just beyond that archway," replied her escort.

A huge elaborately carved arch loomed up before them, and when they had passed it they were entering the great Hyde Park, with its walk ways and carriage-ways for society to display itself.

Ola drew in a quick, delighted breath at the sight of so many gorgeously dressed people in summer colours. Here were the carriages, with coats of arms on their panels, indicating the aristocratic status of those who sat inside.

As they passed they greeted each other with precisely graded nods, so that nobody was insulted by being accorded less acknowledgement than their due, or much worse, more acknowledgement than their due.

How elegant they were, Ola thought. The vehicles gleamed, the horses shone, the coachmen sat proudly. The ladies, under their summer parasols, wore their finery with ease.

Many of them were young girls, out riding with their Mamas, showing themselves at the right time and place so that likely suitors with enough money and status could look them over and consider whether to bid for them. This was clearly one facet of what the Duke had called the marriage mart.

Some of the Mamas waved to him, and imperiously ordered their coachmen to halt, forcing the Duke to draw up beside them. He introduced 'Fraulein Schmidt', whose beauty drew looks of alarm from the women and appreciation from the men.

One carriage was occupied by the Countess of Selbourne, taking the air with her two daughters, her son, Gilbert riding at the rear. The Countess virtually commanded the Duke to ride alongside her, and it seemed as though they would never escape, until Ola had the inspired idea of flirting madly with Gilbert. After that the Duke speedily made his excuses and drew her away.

"He's a spendthrift," he said, sounding annoyed, as they made their way to Rotten Row. "Don't waste your time on him."

"But it wasn't a waste of time," said Ola merrily. "It made you take action, which was the idea."

"Do you mean you deliberately – ?" He stopped, staring at her. She was laughing at him outright.

"Of course," she said.

"Well, I'll be – I suppose I should have expected that."

"So that was the marriage mart?"

"Some of it. It's at its most intense in a ballroom, of course. Oh, how I wish I could take you to the Palace ball. Every man would envy me, and I would like to introduce you to the Queen."

"No, that's not possible," Ola said quickly. "It will be enough if I see her in her carriage. Is this carriage-way the route she will take?"

"Sometimes. And there is Rotten Row, just ahead."

They cantered into the broad avenue where thoroughbred horses could already be seen making their way, bearing their load of thoroughbred humans.

'It is exciting being royal,' Ola thought, 'even though I'm supposed to be pretending not to be. Still, I'm sure it has some disadvantages. If I were really a Princess I would be heavily chaperoned and, and couldn't enjoy a ride like this, alone with him.'

"Why are you not working today?" she asked the Duke.

"I'm playing truant," he answered with a smile. "I was supposed to take some of the royal visitors to see the British Museum, but as I've seen it a dozen times myself I managed to get one of the equerries to take my place."

"That was kind of him," Ola said.

"I had to promise to ask him to shoot with me when the shooting season begins," the Duke said. "As he enjoys coming to stay at my house in the country he agreed at once."

"Tell me some more about your house," Ola begged. "What it is called?"

"Camborne Park. It's been in my family for over five hundred years, and has been owned by twelve generations of my family. It looks a bit like a castle."

"You mean it has towers and turrets?"

"Yes, that's exactly what it has. And an armoury with walls covered with swords and pistols arranged in geometric patterns. There are suits of armour standing in corners.

"My two younger brothers and I used to enjoy playing hide and seek when we were children. We would dart behind the suits of armour and one day we knocked one over. It made a crash that could be heard at the far end of the castle. My father was furious."

"Two younger brothers," she said enviously. "And two sisters, I think you said. How wonderful. It's so sad being an only child."

She was thinking of herself, and was taken aback when he said,

"So Oltenitza has no other Princesses, or Princes?"

"No," she said. "I've had no companionship all my life. It's been very lonely. I envy you, always having someone to play with."

"We fought each other as often as we played," he remembered with a grin. "I used to prefer playing with children from the estate. They always knew the best mischief."

"Oh yes, I'm sure that's true," she said.

As they talked they were making their way along Rotten Row, and the Duke was nodding to acquaintances passing by. Every one of them cast interested eyes over Ola, and several young ladies hailed him in a way that made it impossible for him not to stop.

Mere politeness demanded this, but Ola felt that it was more than politeness that made him flirt with them.

It was, of course, perfectly proper, since it was done under the eyes of the ladies' brothers and fathers, but the Duke enjoyed himself more than Ola liked to see.

On one of the rare occasions that they were alone, she murmered,

"Hmm!"

"I beg your pardon, ma'am."

"I said Hmm! It was intended cynically. You almost made me weep last night with the account of your trials and tribulations in the marriage mart.

"This poor soul, I thought. How he suffers from all these ladies after him! I tell you, sir, what would really make you suffer would be if no woman took the slightest notice of you. And serve you right."

He shouted with laughter.

"You wrong me, ma'am, I'll swear you do."

"I most certainly do not. You're a hardened flirt, drawing moths to your flame, and enjoying every moment of it."

"It's a method of survival, no more. While there are so many, I'm safe, for no woman can accuse me of having paid her particular attention. I developed the idea years ago, when I was little more than a boy and my parents were already pressing 'suitable' brides on me.

"I wasn't in the least interested in filling the nursery. I didn't even want to fall in love. I saw only the disadvantages."

"Which are?"

"Being hung, drawn and quartered," the Duke answered. "Once you're married you can never run away and enjoy yourself. If you do, you know that someone will be hurt and upset simply because you are not there."

"In other words," Ola said, "you don't want to be tied down and you don't want to marry."

"Not until I am so much in love that nothing else matters," the Duke replied.

"And since you avoid being in love, you are condemned to bachelorhood," she said lightly. "I won't say 'a lonely bachelorhood' because it clearly won't be lonely at all. But it will be loveless."

He considered this for a while.

"There have been women in my life, of course there have," he said at last, "but they haven't really meant anything to me. When I said goodbye I found it was easy to forget them."

Ola drew in her breath.

She knew that was what would happen to her.

As he would never see her again, he would soon forget her.

Then he said,

"I am speaking of myself as I was then. Will you believe that – ?"

"Ahoy there! Camborne."

The Duke muttered something impolite beneath his breath as a middle-aged man in military uniform waylaid them. Ola, too, would have wished that this introduction had happened at any other time.

"Introduce me, you dog," the man bawled cheerfully, doffing his hat and bowing at Ola. She inclined her head graciously in return.

"Fraulein, allow me to present General Redbridge. Sir, Fraulein Klara Schmidt."

Ola extended one gloved hand to the General, who bowed low over it. Inexperienced though she was, she had no difficulty in estimating him as a roué.

The Duke seemed to think so too, because he grew increasingly restive at the other man's outrageous compliments. Ola sat there laughing with pleasure, taking none of it seriously.

"If you'll excuse us, General," said the Duke finally. "Fraulein Schmidt has an appointment."

"You're wicked," she teased as they rode on. "I don't have an appointment."

"Yes you do. With me. But not here, because it's too public. Let us complete our ride, and then I'll return you to the hotel to change for our outing this afternoon."

"Where are we going?" she asked eagerly.

"First I'll take you to lunch, and this afternoon we'll do whatever you wish. A shopping trip? Frills and furbelows."

"Oh no! I can shop any time. What I'd really like – " she took a deep breath, unaware that she looked like a bright-eyed child, and that the sight filled him with unaccustomed tenderness.

"Tell me," he said. "Anything you want."

"I want to go on the underground."

"What?" For a moment he was completely taken aback. "You've never – ?"

"Oltenitza is a backward little country compared to this one," she said hastily. "Over there we hear of the wonders to be found in England, and when I return they will expect to be told all about everything."

"Very well. That's where we'll go."

They were in high spirits as he delivered her to the Imperial, and left, promising to be back in an hour. During that hour she and Greta squabbled amiably about the rival merits of a walking dress in deep blue bombazine and one in green velvet.

Ola got her way, and finally sauntered down the stairs in blue, wearing a tiny hat with a small black feather over one eye, and dainty black kid shoes.

His eyes spoke of his admiration. He smiled and took her hand, drawing her quickly out to the waiting vehicle.

This time it wasn't his carriage but a hansom cab that he had hired in the street. This was the kind of detail that Ola was enjoying as much as the major novelties. There were no cabs in Ben Torrach.

"It must be wonderful to be able simply to summon something like this," she said.

"You don't have them in Oltenitza?"

"Not near my home," she said, improvising quickly. "The castle is out in the country, with only a small village nearby, and if I wish to travel I go in the carriage."

"With footmen and outriders?"

"Of course," she said, sounding slightly shocked.

"But it's so cumbersome. This is more convenient."

"It must be difficult not being in the city."

"The country is wild and bleak," she agreed. "But very beautiful." She was describing Ben Torrach now. She had heard somewhere that the countryside in the Balkans was savage and lonely, so her home would do very well as a model.

"There are mountains all around," she went on, warming to her theme. "I have learned to climb them. In my own country I am – what is the word? – *athletisch*."

"Athletic," the Duke replied.

"Ah yes. Thank you. There I am an athletic lady, but not here, because it is not good for ladies."

"English ladies are certainly not expected to be athletic," he agreed. "So, you climb mountains?"

"Oh yes. It is nice to be up so high, where there is wind, and you can get away from people."

"But do you never go into the city?"

"Sometimes, for formal occasions. Sometimes my father goes to see his ministers, sometimes they come to him. Sometimes there are balls and dancing, but too often it is just the same people."

"Do you enjoy dancing?"

"Oh very much. But not when it is so formal. Once I was driving home through the village, and people were dancing in the streets. I forget what they were celebrating, but there was a man playing the violin, and everyone was dancing around him. So I stopped and joined in."

This was all true. Papa had been most displeased.

Suddenly she gasped.

"What is that big, beautiful building?"

"That is Westminster Abbey, where in a few days the

Queen will attend a service of thanksgiving for the fifty years of her reign."

The Duke grinned suddenly.

"I'll tell you a secret. There's a huge argument going on in the Palace. Her advisers want her to wear robes of state and a crown. Her Majesty insists on wearing a bonnet. They're all very upset, but she won't budge."

Ola laughed.

"I think she is right to do what she feels is best. She should not let the great men bully her."

The Duke grinned.

"Nobody bullies the Queen. She's a tiny little woman, about five foot one, but everyone is terrified of her."

"Are you terrified of her?"

"Shaking in my shoes," he said immediately. "Ah, we have arrived."

The cab had swung round Westminster Abbey, and reached the River Thames. The Duke handed her down and paid off the driver.

"Let us walk along the river," he said.

It might have been an accident, but as they strolled along the embankment he contrived to take her hand in his. Ola's heart sang. Whatever might happen in the time ahead, she would always have this moment.

She loved him. She could no longer deny the truth to herself. They had only just met, yet she loved him and she dared to hope that he loved her.

She looked out over the broad expanse of water, enthralled by the way the sunlight sparkled on the ripples. She had never seen such a huge river, such great boats.

The Duke took her to lunch at a small open air restaurant, where they could sit and watch the life of the river. For a while Ola sat watching the great ships and the little boats moving up and down.

"Like the rest of London, the Thames has more visitors than usual just now," said the Duke.

"I have never seen anything like this," Ola said. "So many vessels from so many countries. I did not know that ships could be so big."

"Isn't there a port in your country?"

"Oh no. Oltenitza is land-locked," Ola said quickly, for fear of having to invent a port.

"There's a French ship over there," said the Duke, "and the one coming up the centre of the river is Russian."

Ola looked at the ship and thought it was large but not particularly attractive.

"Do you see many Russians at your court?" the Duke asked.

She gave an eloquent little shudder.

"Please, do not let us speak of them."

She thought that if she was who she was pretending to be, she would dislike the Russians.

But, as she had never met one, she thought it was best to avoid a conversation in which she might show her ignorance.

"As you please," he said. "I'm tired of all that kind of thing, court life, titles, power, bowing and scraping. Sometimes I'd just like to be a plain man at home with my horses."

Ola laughed.

"Why do you laugh?" he challenged her. "Don't you believe me?"

"Of course I don't. I will wager that if you had the choice of being plain mister or a Duke, you would still choose to be a Duke. Am I wrong?"

He looked at her wryly.

"I don't want to answer that," he said. "So let us talk about something else. I would rather talk about you."

"And I want to talk about you," Ola replied. "So we will just have to find something which will please us both, although what it will be, I cannot think."

"I can think of a lot of things," the Duke said, "which I long to say to you and I want to hear your answer. You're so different from anyone I have ever met before. Your Royal Highness – "

"Fraulein Schmidt," she corrected. "The Princess does not exist."

He looked at her quickly.

"I beg your pardon?"

"I mean at this moment she does not exist," she amended quickly. "I want to forget her. I wish I'd never – never been born a Princess."

"I wish that too. It's precisely what causes the trouble between us. You see, there's something – no, never mind."

"If it's important, perhaps you should say it now?"

"It is important, but not for my life could I say it now. Later, when we've had a little time together."

He took her hand in his.

"When do you have to return?" he asked.

"When you grow bored with looking after me."

He shook his head, and spoke in a low voice.

"You know that isn't possible. Why do you pretend not to know?"

"Perhaps there are things we cannot know, cannot allow ourselves to know?" she said with a touch of sadness.

The Duke did not speak. He was looking at her in a way she did not understand. She went on,

"The day will come when you'll have to go back to your ancestral home, and I'll have to go back to mine."

The Duke nodded.

"That is a problem we will have to face sooner or later. But not just at this moment. Let us put all sad things away, and think only of being happy today."

For the rest of the meal they talked of nothing very much, and drank a delicious wine. Now and then they looked up, their eyes met and they smiled.

"Now we'll travel on the underground railway," he said. "And this evening we will find something else to do."

"Don't you have duties?"

"They don't matter, beside you," he said simply.

It was the most totally happy time Ola had ever known.

It did not occur to her then that a terrible danger was looming close to her. A more worldly wise woman would have thought it strange that he could simply drop all his duties to be with her.

But all she saw was the happiness of being with the man she loved, and the conviction that his feelings for her were the same.

Surely, nothing could be wrong in a world where there was love?

They took another cab to Paddington Station and went down a staircase that felt endless until they came out onto a railway platform.

"Where are we?" she asked.

"A long way beneath the earth," he told her, seeing the alarmed look on her face. "Hold onto me."

His arm was about her shoulder, and she took his other hand, squeezing it hard when a train came thundering out of the tunnel. The din was indescribable, and she began to wonder whether she had fallen into hell.

Then they were inside the train, clattering along

through the earth. She tried to talk to him but it was impossible through the noise and at last she gave up.

"Do you want to see any more of the underground?" he asked when they reached a station.

She shook her head. She was beyond speech.

He took her back to Paddington, and they came back up into the light.

"You're looking very pale," he said, looking into her face with concern. "Perhaps I should not have taken you?"

"I wouldn't have missed it for anything," she said. "But I would like a cup of tea."

The Duke chuckled suddenly, and took out a large, white handkerchief.

"I should have said you were pale except for a smut on your nose," he said, rubbing it gently away. "Come now, and we'll find a tea house."

He brought her tea and cream buns, and then they took a cab back to the embankment.

"I have one more surprise for you," he said. "Look."

She followed his pointing finger to a boat hung with coloured lamps. People were scurrying down the gangway, eager for the treat that awaited them. From somewhere came the sound of an accordion.

"You get a trip up the Thames, supper and a little dancing," said the Duke. "And you'll also meet the real Londoners, because these aren't the kind of people we normally share our pleasures with."

He was right. They were not aristocrats, Ola realised, but shopkeepers and servants. They had worked hard all day, and now they were getting ready to play hard. They looked friendly and happy, and suddenly she longed to be one of them.

"Come on," she said, seizing his hand.

They were the last on board. Then the gang plank was pulled up, the propellers whirred, and they were away, heading down river.

All the tables were taken, and many people were milling around eating from a buffet. The head waiter looked nervously at the Duke's elegant clothes, recognising 'the quality'.

"I'll get you a table straight away, sir" he said.

"No, let's stand," said Ola. "I eat just as well on my feet."

"We'll stand," said the Duke with a grin.

They took wine and rolls, went to an upper deck, and stood watching the sun begin to set, while the breeze blew gently round them.

"The perfect end to the perfect day," Ola said contentedly.

"Has it really been a perfect day, Ola?"

"The most perfect of my life."

"And mine," he said. "Because it was spent with you. If only – "

"If only – ?"

He tossed his roll into the water, where it was seized on by seagulls.

"Have you even been in love?" he asked suddenly.

"No." She shook her head.

"That's what I was hoping you would say. And yet – " he sighed. "There is so much that I want to say to you, and yet I can't. If only we weren't – the people that we are."

Now would be a good moment to tell him the truth, she thought.

"John – "

He gave her a quick smile.

"I like to hear you use my name. The others call me Duke, or Camborne, but my name is John, and that's how I like to be with you. Just a man and a woman."

She remembered how he'd said women pursued him for his title, and suddenly she saw the trap she was in. He trusted her to see him as a man because he thought she had a title higher than his own. But if he knew the truth – would he cease to trust her?

A moment ago she had meant to tell him everything, but now the words died unspoken.

"Just a man and a woman," she repeated. "That is all I want us to be."

"I love you," he said.

Her heart soared.

"I love you too," she told him. "I barely know you, and yet I love you."

He touched her face. "We have known each other since the beginning of time."

"And we shall know each other until the end of eternity," she whispered.

Strangely, it seemed that a look of uncertainty passed across his face. He looked down at her hand lying in his, then slowly raised it to his lips.

"I will never forget this moment as long as I live," he said. "Nor shall I cease to treasure it."

Somehow it wasn't quite what she had expected him to say, and she knew a flutter of unease. But surely that was nonsense. He loved her. How could anything be wrong?

CHAPTER FIVE

They sat by the rail for what seemed like hours, watching darkness come down on the river, too happy to speak.

On the way back someone started playing the accordion again, and there was dancing. Laughing, they went to the lower deck and danced until they were giddy. The whole world seemed to be whirling around Ola.

And suddenly she was not dancing any more, but was in his arms, his mouth on hers, and he was kissing her urgently. Between kisses he murmured, "My love, my love."

"My love," she whispered back. "Oh John – John – "

"Tell me that you love me," he begged.

"I love you, I love you."

"Promise me that you'll always remember tonight, and remember that I loved you. Promise me that whatever happens, you'll remember this."

"Why, what a strange thing to say."

"Promise me."

"I promise, I promise."

All too soon it seemed that the boat was tying up at the dock where they had boarded. They found another cab and he gave the driver the address of Ola's hotel.

In the privacy of the cab he kissed her repeatedly, like

a man on the edge of despair. Naïve though she was, she sensed something in his kiss that was more than simply love – a kind of dread, almost anguish.

But she could not think about it. Everything in her was subsumed in pure emotion.

At the hotel he assisted her out and took her inside as far as the stairs.

"I'll be here for you at ten o'clock tomorrow morning," he said.

"Are we going riding?"

"No, not this time. We'll go somewhere where we can have a long talk. Goodnight, my darling."

"Goodnight," she said. "Until tomorrow – my beloved."

She floated upstairs on a cloud of joy. Tomorrow they would have their talk and all would be settled between them. No more deceptions or misunderstandings. Love and happiness lay ahead.

*

The Duke waited until Ola was out of sight. Then the smile faded from his face, and a look of gravity overtook it. A heavy weight seemed to descend on his shoulders, and for a moment there was an expression in his eyes that was almost wretchedness.

Then he straightened his shoulders, turned and went out to the waiting cab.

"Whitehall!" he said curtly.

In twenty minutes he was in the street where so many Government offices were located, and which culminated in the Houses of Parliament. At his instructions the driver halted half way down Whitehall, and the Duke walked into an unobtrusive building with plain doors and windows.

It was a place that would be easy to overlook. There

was no plate on the door to announce its function, nothing to indicate that this was the headquarters of one of the most powerful, yet least known departments of the state.

The Duke went straight up to the third floor and was admitted without question to the office of a plump, pleasant looking man. This was Sir Bernard Danson, the head of the British Secret Service.

He looked up sharply as the Duke entered, and uttered one word.

"Well?"

The Duke shook his head ruefully.

"She's not who she says she is."

"Then who is she?"

"I have no idea. But whatever her true identity, she is not Princess Relola of Oltenitza."

"When did you start to suspect?" Sir Bernard asked.

"From the very first moment, but I've been hoping all the time that she would prove me wrong – maybe turn out to be a real Princess of Oltenitza that we've simply never heard of before, perhaps a cousin of the reigning family?"

Sir Bernard shook his head.

"I've had that matter exhaustively researched, my dear fellow. The Oltenitzan royal family is exactly what we've always known about, King Mathias and Queen Freya, their five daughters, Ludmilla, Sibylla, Myrlene, Flaviola, Helola, and three sons, none of whom is married to a woman called Relola, or has any children of that name.

"Our agents in the field are adamant that the whole family are trapped in Hollentot Castle by a band of Russian soldiers who are keeping them captive, determined not to let any of them reach London."

"But Flaviola – Helola – the similarity of name – "

"Helola is sixteen years old, and I've met Flaviola, one of the ugliest women I've ever seen."

"Then it can't be either of them," the Duke agreed. "But couldn't one of the others have escaped and fled here to ask our help?"

"Then why hasn't she done so? She's been to the Palace, she's met you, a man in the royal service. Has she asked you to introduce her to anyone in Government?"

"No."

"And she's made no attempt to contact her Embassy. I know. Her every movement has been watched, including the long hours she has spent in your company."

"I was doing my duty to my country," the Duke said stiffly, "keeping a suspicious person under observation."

"Very close observation, apparently. All right, my dear fellow. I'm not going to ask awkward questions about how far you felt obliged to go in the Queen's service. It's an occupational hazard, of no importance, as long as you don't lose your head."

Under Sir Bernard's keen eyes, the Duke reddened slightly and said,

"You were saying about the Oltenitzan Embassy. She's been avoiding it. She says she doesn't want them to know she's here because they would envelop her in protocol."

"Or she knows they would expose her. Did she ever try to get access to Her Majesty?"

"Never. I mentioned the lunch for foreign royalty a couple of days ago and suggested that she should be present, and she said she didn't want that. She said it was enough if she could see the Queen at a distance. It was always at a distance."

"Always?"

"Yes, she mentioned it again later, said she'd like to

see Her Majesty driving past in her carriage, but she didn't want to get too close. I see why now. She was afraid of having her silly joke exposed."

"Of course. But look here, Camborne, this could be very serious indeed. We don't know what her agenda is."

"I'm sure it's innocent. It's a game to her, no more."

"You don't think she's got anything serious in mind?"

"Of course not. The sheer clumsiness of the pretence proves its innocence. Why, she even told me that Oltenitza was a land locked country, which it isn't. She told me she was an only child, whereas we know the Oltenitzan royal family is large.

"She hasn't bothered to learn the simplest thing about the place. If she were a spy, which I take it is what you're suggesting, she'd be far more professional."

"Yes, I dare say you're right. But she's got to be stopped. We can't have young women running around London pretending to be royalty from a friendly foreign power. It could lead to unfortunate – er – misunderstandings."

"I see that. I'll talk to her."

"No, bring her to me. Let's see if I can persuade her to go back to where she came from and stop being such a ninny."

"You won't be hard on her?"

"Good grief, what do you take me for? I've got daughters. In fact, you've met them."

The Duke had been hoping Sir Bernard would not say that. He had indeed met the Danson daughters on a weekend visit to their home, and endured their mother's determination to thrust them to his attention. His good manners had constrained him to remain for the whole weekend, but he had finally escaped with a sigh of relief, feeling that he had only just got out alive.

He knew now why no other woman had claimed his heart. He had been waiting for Ola to flame across his horizon. Soon any barriers between them would be down, and he could ask her to marry him.

He was a happy man when he went home that night.

*

The Duke was waiting for Ola at the foot of the stairs next morning, in exactly the same position as he had left her. His eyes lit up at the sight of her, just as she knew her own must have done at the sight of him.

"Where are we going?" she asked smiling at him.

"For a walk in the park. Not Hyde Park this time, but Green Park, which is just over the road."

At first it seemed just a pleasant walk through beautiful gardens, but even then she was aware of a strange tension in him.

Suddenly he said,

"My darling, do you trust me?"

"Of course I trust you," she said at once.

"Do you believe that I love you?"

"If you tell me that you do, I believe it."

"And I tell you that I love you with my whole heart, and I always will. I love and I trust you, and I beg you to trust me enough to tell me the truth."

"The truth?" she asked cautiously. "About what?"

"About who you really are. I know you're not a Princess," he replied.

Her heart seemed to skip a beat.

"You do?"

"Darling, I know that it's all a pretence. I realise it's just a game to you, but it's a very dangerous game. How could you be so incautious as to choose a real country? Didn't you realise that we could check on the royal family of

Oltenitza?"

"You mean there's really a – ?" She stopped, realising what she had given away.

"Yes, there's really an Oltenitza. Don't tell me you didn't know."

"But I didn't. I made it up, I swear I did."

"How could you?" he enquired.

"I don't know – it just came to me. How could I have imagined a real name? I've never heard of it."

"Most people hadn't until recently. Then it was in the newspapers once or twice. The royal family are trapped in their castle by Russian soldiers. You must have seen it and noticed it, without realising."

"Oh my goodness! There really is such a place." She pressed her hands to her cheeks and gave a little laugh. "Fancy that! Oh, I've been such a fool!"

"What kind of game were you playing? Where do you really come from?"

"Scotland. My name is Ola McNewton. Papa and I were going to come to London for the Jubilee, but he died. He made me promise to come anyway, and I – I just thought it would be fun to be someone else. I was so bored with being me. Can you understand that?"

"Of course I can," he said tenderly. "I can even see that it's amusing. No wonder you didn't want any contact with the Embassy. But my dear girl, can you imagine the chaos you've caused? We thought one of the family must have escaped from the castle and reached England, and we've been going crazy trying to work out the truth."

Her hand flew to her mouth.

"Oh dear, I'm so sorry. I didn't mean to cause any trouble. I just wanted to enjoy myself, and think of Papa. You see, in some ways I've felt I was doing it for him. He was very sentimental about the Queen. A long time ago he

71

was a little bit in love with her."

"What?"

"He was in the army then, and a whole group of officers were invited to a ball at Balmoral. He danced with the Queen, several times. In those days he had a very strong Scottish accent, and she had to make him repeat everything twice. He was starry-eyed about her all the rest of his life. Mama used to tease him about it, not minding at all, of course, because they loved each other so much.

"He said it would be nice to see her again, just from a distance. And when he died recently, I was going to see her for him."

The Duke regarded her with a rueful grin.

'Wait until Danson hears this,' he thought, shaking his head. 'Innocence personified.'

He took her hand between his.

"Come with me," he said. "I want you to talk to a friend of mine, and then we'll put this business behind us, and think of the future."

"The future, John?"

He smiled and carried her hand to his lips.

"Come," he said.

They took a cab to Whitehall and were instantly admitted to see Sir Bernard Danson.

He listened to the story, which they told between them, with an ironic smile on his amiable face.

"And how about 'Lady Krasler'?" he asked. "Who is she?"

"That's Greta Lanso, my maid. She came to look after me and make sure I didn't get into any trouble."

"I have never heard such a farrago in all my days!" Sir Bernard said. "What were you thinking of, young woman?"

"I know I haven't been very sensible," she admitted.

72

"It was only a prank that went wrong."

"A prank? Well, well, let's leave it at that. Let me have a statement in writing and we'll say no more. Yes, Hawkins, what is it?"

He had looked up as a soberly dressed clerk entered the room. There was no sign in his manner that this had been pre-arranged between them.

"Excuse me, Sir Bernard, there's a message for the Duke of Camborne."

"Yes?" said the Duke, rising.

"It's from Lord Baisley," said the clerk, naming the Queen's Comptroller. "Your Grace is wanted at the Palace without delay."

"You'd better be off," said Sir Bernard. "If you're not back when Miss McNewton is ready to leave, I'll send her to the Imperial in a cab."

The Duke smiled at Ola.

"I'll return as soon as I can."

"Don't worry," she said. "I'm all right."

She watched him, smiling, until the door had closed behind him. Then she turned back to face Sir Bernard, and the smile died from her face.

His own face had been stripped of its amiability, leaving only a cold mask behind.

"Now," he said, and the word seemed to freeze the air. "Now, we'll have the truth out of you."

"But I've told you the truth."

He made a sound of contempt.

"Please madam, those pretty tales will do for Camborne, but I've been around a lot longer than he has. You're a spy. The only question is – for whom? You'll tell me sooner or later, so why not save us all a lot of time?"

"But it's not true," she cried, rising from her seat.

73

"I've told you the truth."

"Who do you work for?"

"I'm not a spy," she insisted.

"Who do you work for?"

"But you said you understood – "

"Who do you work for?"

Terror overcame her. She ran to the door and tried to pull it open, but it was now locked.

"Let me out!" she screamed, hammering on the door. "John! *John!*"

"He's gone," said Sir Bernard. "He won't come back for you."

"John!" she screamed again. "Where are you?"

"You stupid girl, what are you expecting? He's done his part in getting you here quietly and without a fuss. You won't see him again."

She turned horrified eyes on him.

"His part?" she whispered.

"The Duke saw through you the first day and reported to me, since when you've been under surveillance. He has questioned you on my behalf to try to gauge the extent of your activities, and finally he brought you to us."

"I don't believe you," she choked.

"Don't you? Let me tell you something about those meetings when you were weaving your arts about him. You thought he was coming under your spell, didn't you? But last night the Duke stood in this very room and said to me, 'I was doing my duty to my country, keeping a suspicious person under observation.'"

"He wouldn't betray me like that," she choked.

Sir Bernard gave an unpleasant bark of laughter.

"Betray you? Madam, is it possible to betray you? A spy, a deceiver, a trickster? It is you who betray, and now you have been found out. His Grace is totally loyal to the British throne, so abandon any further idea of ensnaring him with your wiles."

"*No!*" she screamed. "It isn't true. I'm not a spy."

"You are a spy, madam, and you're probably an assassin too. Oh yes, Camborne told me how often you asked to see the Queen, but always from a safe distance. How big a distance, I wonder. Not too far for an accurate shot at Her Majesty. And then, of course, you'd have had to dispose of poor Camborne himself. But on whose behalf?"

"It's not true, it's not true." The words were barely audible. Darkness was engulfing her.

"Sooner or later you will tell me who you work for. Unless your confederate breaks first."

"My – confederate?"

"The woman posing as your lady-in-waiting, whom you have so obligingly named as Greta Lanso. I'm obliged to you for that, as she has refused to say a word since her arrest."

"Arrest?"

"She was picked up at your hotel an hour ago and is now behind bars. She will talk, and you will talk. You can take my word for that."

She knew then that the nightmare was real.

*

At Buckingham Palace the Duke went straight to Lord Baisley's office.

"I came as soon as I received your message," he said.

"Message? I sent no message."

"Surely you did. I was with Sir Bernard and someone came in to say – " his voice ran down and a look of horror came into his eyes.

"I don't believe it," he said. "It isn't possible."

75

"What isn't possible?" asked Lord Baisley.

But he was talking to thin air. The Duke had left the room at a run.

He found a cab quickly and shouted, "as fast as you can go." It seemed an eternity until he reached Whitehall, and for all that time he was telling himself that there must have been a mistake.

But in his heart he knew that there had been no mistake. Suddenly he recalled tales of how Sir Bernard's bluff amiability was a mask hiding something more sinister. He had never seen that side of the man himself, regarding him as a bit of a buffoon. Now he saw how he had been duped into leaving Ola alone with him. But he might still be wrong.

Until the last moment he clung to the hope that he would arrive to find that all was well. That hope died in the first moment of seeing Danson's face.

"What have you done with her?" the Duke demanded savagely.

"Put her behind bars, where she belongs. Forgive me for that little stratagem, but it wouldn't have done to have you here, making a scene. As it was, she screamed the place down, banging on the door, shrieking for you to come and save her."

"Dear God!" the Duke whispered, feeling the hairs on the back of his neck stand up in horror.

The picture of Ola screaming in terror, begging him to save her, finding herself abandoned, was more than he could bear.

"It was most distressing," said Danson with a shudder. "I had hoped to get the business over without disturbance, but I'm afraid she's going to cause a lot of trouble."

"Are you out of your mind!" the Duke shouted. "You can't believe this nonsense."

"My dear fellow, it was you who gave me the evidence against her of how often she asked to see the Queen from a distance."

"So that she wouldn't be exposed – "

"So that she could get a safe shot."

Into the Duke's mind came the memory of Ola saying, 'I'm an excellent shot. I can hit a bull's eye at fifty paces,' and then hastily retreating, denying what she had just admitted.

Like someone who had inadvertently revealed too much.

Everything in him howled NO! It wasn't possible.

And yet – ?

He became aware that Danson was still talking.

"And when she'd shot the Queen, she'd have shot you. She would have to if she wanted to get away. You're lucky to be alive, so don't start getting sentimental about her.

"Just stay out of it from now on. It wouldn't look good if you were to try to defend a woman like that. In a short time she'll be tried, convicted and executed. And that will be the end of her."

CHAPTER SIX

Ola had no idea where she was, except that there were bars on the windows and a tiny barred window in the door. The walls were stone, the bed was narrow and hard.

She knew nothing of Greta's fate, except that she had been brought to a place like this. Her companion had bravely maintained silence, but soon she would learn that her mistress had told them her name. This apparent treachery would break her heart.

Nobody would tell her where Greta was. In fact, nobody would speak to her at all. Sometimes a face would appear at the bars in the door, but if she called out they ignored her.

She was alone, with nobody to care what happened to her.

When she thought of how the Duke had betrayed her she wanted to cry and cry until there were no tears left. He had won her love with his charm, his tenderness, his strength. And it had all been false. While he seemed to be adoring her, he had been observing her as a 'suspicious person'.

She paced the floor until she was exhausted, then sat on the bed, pressed up into the corner, laid her head on her knees, and folded her arms protectively.

She stayed like this for hours, sometimes dozing,

sometimes waking to the sound of doors slamming and distant cries. It was like being in hell, deprived of all hope.

In the morning she was brought a meal of bread and cold water. The wardress slammed it down, gave her a look of contempt, and departed, slamming the door.

Sir Bernard Danson had told her she would be interrogated again, and at every sound outside her door she braced herself. But it was not until the afternoon that footsteps stopped, the key turned and the door swung open.

Bracing herself, she turned defiantly to face the wardress.

But it was not a wardress.

It was the last man in the world she expected to see.

"You?" she whispered. "You dare to come and face me?"

"You should be glad that I did," said the Duke through gritted teeth. "I'm not supposed to be here. I've been warned off taking any further interest in you. Your guards have orders to keep me out. I managed to bribe them but I don't have much time."

He came close to her, looking down into her ravaged face with terrible eyes.

"Tell me it isn't true," he said hoarsely. "The things they're saying about you can't be true – *tell me!*"

"What is the use of telling you?" she demanded. "They things *they* are saying about me are the things *you* said. *You* accused me. *You* brought me here."

"You brought yourself here," he raged. "Did you really imagine you could put on such a performance and nobody would be surprised?

"You came right to the doors of Buckingham Palace, a place where details of every royal family in the world are kept. You walked in and challenged us all to spot you as an impostor. I was suspicious from the first moment."

"So you 'kept me under observation'?"

"Yes," he snapped.

"That was all you were doing? All those things you said – "

"Let us not speak of them," he said roughly. "I did my duty."

"Your duty? It was your duty to kiss me and say that you loved me? It was your duty to – ?"

"That's enough. It's not for you to demand explanations of me. You came here to deceive."

"And I failed. But your deception was very successful, wasn't it? Right up to the moment when you told that man I was behaving suspiciously."

"Which you were. You didn't want to get close to the Queen, but you wanted to see her from a distance. With a gun, according to Danson."

"You can't believe that."

"Why not? You told me you were a crack shot – until you checked yourself and took it back."

"But that – I just thought it wasn't ladylike."

She had wanted him to love her, but she could not say that now. Looking into his grim face, she saw no yielding.

"Is that the best explanation you can offer?" he demanded coldly.

"Yes, it's the best explanation I can offer. It's the truth. I've been stupid, but nothing more. And the stupidest thing of all – " she broke off as her voice wobbled.

How could she tell this iron man that the stupidest thing of all was to have believed his honeyed words and given him her heart, given it so completely that it was still his, even though part of her was close to hating him.

How he would laugh at that!

"Yes?" he demanded. "What is the stupidest thing of all?"

Suddenly she was too weary to go on.

"It doesn't matter," she said. "You wouldn't believe me. After this you would never believe anything that I said, any more than I could believe you."

In the cold stone cell, they faced each other in silence.

The Duke walked over to the window and looked out as far as he could. The bleakness of the surroundings suffocated him. He ought to go. There was no more to say. Yet he could not bear to leave her.

"I think you do me an injustice," he said curtly. "Was it I who created this situation?"

"No, I began it by coming to London in a disguise. But when I look back on some of the talks we've had, I can see that the things I said, which you have used to accuse me – "

"Well?" he snapped.

"You invited me to say those things, John. You laid traps for me – "

"Because I knew you to be a deceiver," he raged, infuriated by this injustice. "I merely wanted to know how much of a deceiver."

"And then you went to Sir Bernard Danson and told him what you had discovered."

He was silent, gazing at her with burning eyes.

"Tell me," she went on, "was he one of the 'friends' who warned you off helping me?"

"Yes. He thinks you were going to kill the Queen, then kill me? Is that true?"

Suddenly her temper flared. It might be unwise to antagonise him, but she was beyond thinking of that. The bitter, searing anger that had been consuming her from the start flamed out into the open.

"Would I admit it, if it were true?" she flung at him.

He took two strides towards her, seized her shoulders and gave them a shake.

"Tell me the truth," he shouted. "Has it all been lies? Every smile, every kiss – all a pretence, leading to murder?"

"Whose life do you care about, John?" she asked recklessly. "The Queen's or your own?"

"The Queen's. Only hers, because if you are false to me, I'll put the gun in your hand myself and invite you to shoot me. What would I care for life then?"

He closed his eyes in horror as it came back to him forcefully that it was not his life under threat, but hers. By this time next week she might be dead, and his life a blasted wasteland.

Opening his eyes he saw her face turned up to his, the dark shadows around the eyes, the mouth tense with exhaustion and horror. He recalled her on the first day, the high-spirited brilliance with which she had played her part, the young, eager laughter with which she had confronted the world.

All brought to this.

With a groan he tightened his arms and covered her mouth with his own, seeking to find the secret of her heart. Her lips were sweet against his, as sweet as in the other kisses they had shared, and for a moment the dreadful surroundings vanished, leaving only the two of them.

"Ola," he murmured, "Ola – "

For a moment she succumbed to the magic that was still there in his kiss, even now. In his arms she could forget everything.

But only briefly.

The next moment he said the words that broke the spell.

"Tell me the truth," he begged. "Tell me, Ola – "

She began to struggle against him.

"No," she said fiercely. "Let me go. It's over. Don't you know that?"

As he was forced to release her he saw that she was right. Suddenly everything was darkness in his mind.

"Sir Bernard thinks of everything," she said. "He couldn't get me to say what he wanted to hear yesterday, so he sends you to do his dirty work. I said you'd laid traps for me. I didn't think you'd try to lay another."

"No!" His cry was anguished. "That's not true, I swear it."

"Leave me!" she ordered him. "Don't come back. I've told you the truth. That's all I can do."

"Ola – "

"Leave me, I say!"

Despairing, he turned away to the door, but with a swift movement she reached out and touched him.

"Wait," she said. "I have one thing to ask, not for myself, but for Greta. I may have been stupid and brought this on myself, but her only crime is to be loyal to me. I am no spy, and neither is she, but she's been locked up too.

"For pity's sake, get her out. Never mind me, but save her. Promise me that you will."

"I'll try," he said. "But I don't know what lies in my power."

"Save her. Don't let her suffer for my sake."

He was frowning. "I don't know what – perhaps I can seek help from my godmother."

"Anything," she said. "Just set her free. It doesn't matter about me."

He gave her a look and left without another word.

Time dragged past. At every step outside her door she

stiffened, but only once did somebody enter, and that was the wardress to escort her to a small bathroom nearby where she was able to wash for the first time since yesterday. When she returned to her cell there was a glass of water and a bowl of soup.

She replayed the scene with the Duke endlessly, wondering why she had been so rash as to lose her temper with the one man who might have helped her.

But she could not have helped it. Bitterness and misery had risen up to overwhelm her, and the stinging words had poured out. She regretted it now more for Greta's sake than her own. If only she could help Greta, or even see her.

She discounted the Duke's words about his godmother. They were a device to silence her while he escaped. How could his godmother help?

As the hours wore on, and she thought of the worst that could happen, she dropped her head in her hands and wept.

At last there were more footsteps that stopped outside the door. The key turned. Had the time come for her interrogation?

"They're ready for you now," said the grim faced wardress who had come in. "Hurry up! They've got better things to do than be kept waiting by the likes of you."

The wardress walked her down a long corridor and into a small room at the end. Two men in black clothes rose at the sight of her and indicated for her to follow them out of a far door. She looked this way and that, but there was no means of escape.

Then they were out in a small, ugly yard, where a closed carriage stood. One of them indicated for her to get in, and when she did so they sat one each side of her.

"For pity's sake, where are you taking me?" she

begged.

"We're just doing as we're told, miss," one of them said woodenly. "Keep away from the window."

With the thick blinds down she had no way of knowing where she was. They seemed to travel for a long time, and she tried to remember the journey yesterday, when she had been brought here. That had seemed like an eternity.

At last they stopped. As she got out she realised that she was in another courtyard, but this one was elegant and well built. She had no time to look around before she was directed through a door and into a corridor. It was plain but clean and pleasant – not a prison, she thought.

They walked for a long time, through corridors that grew lighter and better furnished, then through rooms with thick carpets and luxurious furniture.

Still Ola did not know where she was, but she knew it was not the place in Whitehall where she had been before. It was too much like a palace.

A palace!

"Is this – ?"

"Just keep going, miss."

They had reached a little ante-room, furnished with chairs upholstered in crimson damask. On the wall was a small mirror with a gilt frame. The sight of herself horrified Ola. Despite her attempts to tidy up in the bathroom, her hair was dishevelled. She had slept in her clothes, and looked it.

But it was more than untidy clothes. She had been through hell and her face showed it. There was no beauty there that she could see. Just a pale, tortured woman drowning in misfortune and anguish.

One of the men pointed ahead.

"You go through that door," he said.

There was nothing to tell her what she would find on

the other side.

She pushed open the door slowly and went into a poorly lit room. It seemed to be very large, and furnished with dark oak furniture. Red crimson curtains hung at the window, and a deep red patterned carpet covered the floor.

At the far end was a desk at which sat a little old lady, absorbed in writing something. She was tiny, and dressed in black except for a snowy white cap on her head, from which long streamers floated down her back.

At first the little woman seemed unaware that anyone had entered the room. Then she raised her head, revealing a plump face and little eyes.

Ola gasped.

It was the face in the official photograph that she had seen in the Imperial Hotel.

"Your Majesty!" she said, dropping into a deep curtsey.

She stayed there for what seemed like ages, until at last she heard the Queen say,

"Hmm! All right, get up."

She did so. Queen Victoria looked her up and down with a disconcerting shrewdness in her eyes. When she spoke, the words were shocking.

"So you're the spy who's trying to assassinate me?"

"No," Ola said frantically. "That's not true – " she drew in a sharp breath as something dawned on her. "And Your Majesty knows it's not true."

"Indeed? How do I?"

"Because you see me alone, and kept your eyes down while I walked across the floor. If you thought I was dangerous you would never have taken your eyes off me."

"Hmm! And you think that proves you innocent?"

"No, Your Majesty. It merely proves that you believe

me innocent."

"Not necessarily. If you'd tried to attack me I think my godson would have protected me." The Queen raised her voice. "You'd better show yourself, John."

The Duke stepped out from behind the hangings.

Ola stared at him.

His godmother! Of course! Why had she not realised?

The next moment she fainted.

She awoke to find herself lying on a sofa, with the Queen of England sitting beside her, tenderly dabbing her forehead with a scented, lace handkerchief.

"Good," she said briskly when she saw Ola's eyes open. "John, has that tea arrived?"

"The footman is just bringing it now, ma'am."

Ola knew she was dreaming when she felt herself being supported by the Duke, while the Queen held a cup of tea to her lips.

"Now," said the Queen seating herself and regarding Ola sternly, "John has told me the most incredible story I have ever heard, and he has sworn to me that, unlikely as it looks, you are innocent. For my own part, I do not regard impersonating royalty as innocent."

"It was only meant as a joke, Your Majesty."

"Nor do I regard it as a joke."

"It was just that I've lived such a dull life, and my father always talked about you so much."

The Queen frowned.

"Who was your father?"

"Colonel Owen McNewton. Of course, he was only a Captain when you met him."

"I met him? When?"

"Years ago. At Balmoral. Your Majesty was there one

87

summer with Prince Albert, and you gave a ball. He was invited, along with several other officers, and you danced with him. He said you had to keep asking him to repeat himself because you couldn't understand his Scottish accent."

The Queen was staring at her.

"That handsome young man was your father?"

"Yes, ma'am. He was very honoured that, despite his accent, you danced with him three times."

Suddenly the Queen let out a shriek of laughter. It was so unexpected that they both stared at her.

"Oh yes, I did. Three times. You see, he was so very good looking, quite the handsomest man in the room, and I was rather cross with dear Albert that evening. I thought it wouldn't do any harm to make him a little bit jealous."

"Ma'am!" said the Duke. "I'm shocked."

"Did it make him jealous, Your Majesty?" asked Ola.

"Oh yes, very. But he didn't react like any other man. Not a word of anger. He simply engaged Captain McNewton in conversation, and kept him talking all the rest of the evening. He never would tell me what they had talked about."

"Coburg, ma'am," said Ola. "His Royal Highness told Papa all about his home, and made it sound so delightful that the following year my father took a trip there, and met my mother."

The laughter died from the Queen's face.

"Is that really true?"

"Yes, ma'am."

"Your mother came from Coburg?"

"Yes, ma'am."

The Queen was silent for a moment. When she next spoke, it was in German.

"Did your mother ever speak to you about her homeland?"

"A great deal," said Ola in the same language. She understood that this was a test. "She never saw it again and she missed it so much. She said it was the loveliest place in the world."

Queen Victoria nodded, and spoke in English.

"Yes," she said sadly. "You have the true Coburg accent. Ah, how long ago it was! And how happy we were! John tells me that your father is dead now."

"Yes ma'am. He never really got over my mother's death. They were everything to each other."

"Yes," said the Queen sadly. "Oh yes."

There was no mistaking the look on her face. She was thinking of her beloved Albert, and how all the festivity and the adulation meant nothing without him.

For a moment the other two had a glimpse of a love that had survived death and separation, and long, lonely years. And they knew that nothing really mattered to Victoria except the time to come, when she and her Albert would be together again.

It was a love such as they themselves might have known, if things had been different. But now everything had changed.

"So you're Owen McNewton's daughter," said the Queen at last. "And you had this absurd idea that you could be a Princess."

"I didn't mean to pick a real country ma'am. I didn't know there was such a place."

"Yes, John has told me. But Oltenitza exists and is in trouble. The royal family has been trapped in their castle by a group of Russian soldiers. So, naturally your arrival here has puzzled the Russians, as well as the English. And we need to keep them puzzled."

"But how, ma'am? Everyone knows about me now."

"No, only we know about you, and that is how it must stay. From now on, everything you do must be under expert guidance."

It took a moment for the implications of this to dawn on Ola.

"Do you mean that I am to continue being – I mean, pretending to be – ?"

"Certainly, but this time you will be supported by my recognition. You will be presented to me, and I will greet you as an Oltenitzan Princess. Let anyone dare to doubt you, then!"

As Ola was too dumbstruck to speak the Duke asked,

"Have you decided which Princess she shall be ma'am?"

"Either Flaviola or Helola, but she will be known simply as Princess Ola. The Russians can simply wonder which one she is, and if there has to be an explanation eventually, we'll invent a distant cousin."

The Queen smiled kindly at Ola.

"Now you must go back to your hotel, and one of my own ladies will attend you and instruct you in the details. In public, the Duke here will escort you. Go and get some sleep now, and tomorrow he will bring you here to be officially presented to me."

"And Greta?" Ola asked quietly.

"Who?"

"Greta Lanso, my maid who was arrested with me, and who is still in that terrible place. If I am innocent, so is she. When will she be released, please?"

"All in good time," said the Queen.

Ola raised her head and looked Her Majesty firmly in the eye.

"No, ma'am, that isn't good enough. I won't leave her there."

A chill settled over the Queen's face. She was not used to people telling her that her decisions were not good enough.

"Young woman," she said at last, "let us be plain about this. Your innocence is very far from being proved, and so is hers.

"You've been given a chance to redeem yourself, and if you do well we may reconsider the question of your innocence, and what is to happen to you. But the same does not apply to her."

"But I need her," Ola cried. "I can't do this without her."

"I've told you, you will have one of my ladies."

"Greta is my maid, and my friend. She can help me in ways that nobody else can. The whole plan will have a better chance of success if Greta is with me."

"My answer is no," replied the Queen firmly.

"Your Majesty, I beg you to release her. She's only in trouble because of me and I won't live in comfort while she's in that place."

"You have no choice."

"Oh, but I do. I won't do this without her."

The Queen gave Ola a long, hard look.

"Do you realise what you are saying? Are you prepared to be sent back to the cells? Is that what you want?"

"No, ma'am, it's not what I want. It terrifies me to think of being sent back there. But I'll go, rather than abandon a faithful friend who is suffering because of me."

The words were defiant but her voice was small and

shaking. When she had finished, she closed her eyes in dread at what she might have brought down upon herself.

And so she did not see the look of satisfaction that the Queen gave to the Duke, or the slight smile that touched her lips.

"Very well," said Queen Victoria at last. "It seems that I must yield. You and I will talk more tomorrow after your presentation. You must leave me, now. I'll send a message to Sir Bernard about your maid. John will see you to your hotel."

She rang a bell on her desk and a woman appeared.

"Lady Cadwick will take care of you until the carriage is ready."

She waited until Ola had left the room under Lady Cadwick's care, before saying,

"She is everything you told me, my dear boy. Loyal and true. I think she would really have gone back to her cell rather than betray her friend."

"I'm sure of it, ma'am."

"She'll make you an excellent wife."

But the Duke shook his head. "I fear there's no chance of that. I think she almost hates me now."

"What? After all you did for her, bursting in on me in that rude fashion and refusing to leave until I'd heard you out?"

"I owed her that after betraying her so carelessly to that fool, Danson. I had no idea he had such a lurid imagination.

"But I'm afraid it's too late for Ola and myself ma'am. We've said such things to each other – "

He sighed.

"I don't know what can happen now," he said heavily.

"It will come right if you truly love each other," said the Queen. "And that love is worth fighting for. Nothing is more worth it. Always remember that."

CHAPTER SEVEN

After another cup of strong tea, Ola began to feel a little better and with Lady Cadwick's help, she tidied up her hair. When she left the Palace half an hour later, her dishevelled clothes were concealed by a velvet cloak.

One of the Queen's carriages was waiting for her, its large coat of arms on the panel proclaiming that this person travelled under Her Majesty's protection.

The Duke was waiting for her beside the carriage. He offered his hand to assist her, and she took it because her legs were shaky, but as soon as she was inside she released it and huddled in the far corner, as far away from him as possible.

When he was inside and closed the door, the carriage began to rumble away out of the Palace yard.

"Ola – " he said, reaching for her.

"Please – " She flung out a hand to ward him off. "I want to say that I – that I am deeply sensible of what I owe you. When you spoke of asking help from your godmother I did not realise – "

"That I meant the Queen. Yes, she has always been very good to me."

"And of course you interceded on my behalf," she said, speaking with an effort. "That was kind of you."

"Please, Ola, there's no need – "

"I – would not like you to think – that I was ungrateful – but – "

It was too much for her. She dropped her head into her hands and burst into violent sobs. At once he was beside her, trying to put his arms about her.

"Ola, darling – please – "

"No," she said fiercely. "I will do as Her Majesty wishes, for as long as she needs, but – anything else – "

"I know," he said sadly. "You think you cannot trust me – "

"Nor you me."

"Would I have taken you to the Queen if I didn't trust you?"

"Oh, you know I'm not a spy, but that isn't what I meant."

"No, of course not. I realise that it's hard, but can't we find our way back to each other if we try?"

She raised her head. In the dim light of the carriage, he could see the tears glittering on her cheeks, and the urge to take her in his arms was almost overwhelming. But he knew he must resist it, at least for the moment.

"No," she whispered through her tears. "It's over. Whatever we might have had, died before it had a chance to truly live. It can never flourish now."

He wanted to deny this vehemently, but he knew she would need all her courage for the time ahead, and he must help her by offering her his strength to lean on, without pressing his own wishes on her.

There were some curious eyes as she entered the hotel, leaning on the Duke's arm, and she wondered how much was known about Greta's abrupt departure that morning.

"Greta," she murmured. "Is she here yet?"

He approached the desk and murmured something.

"She is here," he said when he returned. "I've told them you've both been in an accident. Take my arm and we'll go upstairs."

At her door he knocked and Greta immediately answered.

"Where is she?" she asked angrily. "Where – oh, my darling!"

Ola stumbled forward into Greta's arms and the two women clung to each other.

The Duke quietly closed the door and went away.

*

Neither woman expected to sleep much that night, but both were mistaken, and when they woke next morning they were sufficiently refreshed to feel stronger, and able to face the world.

Over breakfast they discussed their experiences, and Ola found much there to horrify her.

"They said you had 'confessed everything'," Greta said. "They had my name and said you had given it to them, so I must betray you in return."

"Dearest Greta, forgive me. I did tell them your name, but that was in all innocence, before I realised what they meant to do. How could I have guessed?"

"You couldn't. I thought it must have been something like that. They will not turn us against each other."

There was no time for more talk because Lady Cadwick arrived with maids, and several costumes suitable for court presentation. Each one was white and elaborate, with a long train.

Ola donned gown after gown, walking up and down before the long mirror, while the others squabbled amiably about which one suited her the best. At last they settled on an elegant white silk and lace, heavily draped over the bustle, and with a train that was three yards long.

"The train may be a little difficult," Lady Cadwick explained. "When you have been presented to Her Majesty, you will have to back away without tripping over the train."

They tried it, and Ola tripped over four times before she found the trick of it.

To complete the elaborate ensemble she wore a long white veil, held in place by a coronet of diamonds which Lady Cadwick loaned her from the fabulous Cadwick collection. On top of this were fixed three ostrich feathers. In addition she had a large feathered fan, and long white gloves.

Ola had wanted to be presented at court. It had never occurred to her that it would be like this!

Lady Cadwick stood back and looked at her with pride. Then she dropped a deep curtsey.

"Your Royal Highness!" she said.

"Will I get away with it?"

"Oh yes, you will, I promise. You look magnificent and just as you ought. Now, you are all ready to be presented."

She was to be Ola's sponsor, for no lady could be presented at court without being introduced by another lady who had, herself, been presented. They travelled to the Palace in the Cadwick carriage, its ancient coat of arms emblazoned on the side.

It was a very fine day, and the carriage was open, so that everyone in the streets could see Princess Ola on her way to be received by the Queen.

Her last arrival at Buckingham Palace had been at the rear. Now she drove in splendour through the front gate and under the central arch into the courtyard beyond.

From the moment the carriage stopped everything was done with great ceremony. Powdered footmen stepped forward to open the door. Ola descended very carefully and stood while Lady Cadwick checked to see that everything was right.

Then they entered the Palace and began the long walk up crimson carpeted staircases, along broad corridors, until they came to the room that she had first seen in the Duke's company only a few days ago, when he had told her all about presentations.

She had reached the sitting room where, he had said, the debutantes waited for their turn. Lady Cadwick ushered her in.

The next moment she had a shock.

The Duke was there, watching the door with painful anxiety.

At first Ola thought that he looked right through her.

Then he became tense.

"I did not recognise you," he said, speaking awkwardly. "You look very splendid – Your Royal Highness."

How she would once have loved the astounded look in his eyes as he saw her glory. What joy there would have been in his admiration as he saw her more beautiful than ever before!

But not now.

A chasm yawned between them.

"Good afternoon, Duke," she said courteously. "As you can see, I'm playing my part. Do you have any advice for me? I realise that your special knowledge is valuable."

"Be hostile to me if you wish," he sighed. "But don't let it take your mind off your job. In a few moments the Oltenitzan ambassador will be here. He knows everything and wants to help us, for the sake of his country. He will assist you all he can."

She inclined her head, moving with excessive care lest she dislodge the ostrich feathers which waved wildly with every movement.

She thought the Duke himself was looking splendid in court dress of white knee breeches and ceremonial sword. Ola was sure no man had ever looked so handsome.

He left the room and returned after a moment with a thin, middle-aged man with a worried expression, whom he introduced as the Oltenitzan ambassador. He gave Ola a deep, respectful bow.

"Your Royal Highness," he said, loud enough for all to hear. Then, lowering his voice, he murmured, "I am deeply grateful for everything you are doing to help our poor country."

"I am very happy to help you in any way I can," she said politely.

"Then if you would be so kind as to wear this."

He opened a small box on which lay a diamond studded decoration.

"It is the Grand Order of Oltenitza, First Class. All our Princesses have it, and I hope you will accept it with our gratitude."

She smiled her pleasure, Lady Cadwick pinned it on to her shoulder, and everything was complete. There was a bustle of movement. It was time for everyone to take their place.

"You'll be the third to go," the Duke told Ola. "Don't be afraid."

"I am not afraid," Ola said quietly.

"No, I don't think you are," he said, and his voice was warm. "You won't fail at the mouth of the lion's den."

She gave a wan smile. "There are worse lions' dens than this," she reminded him.

He nodded. For a moment his hand clasped hers. Then he drew the ambassador away, leaving the debutantes and their sponsors preparing for their great moment.

Ola tried to concentrate on what she was doing, but all she could think of was the feel of his hand on hers.

Then it was her turn. The double doors were thrown open, revealing the crowded throne room beyond. Lady Cadwick and Ola moved into the doorway, where Lady Cadwick handed a card to the lord in waiting, who read aloud,

"Her Royal Highness, Princess Ola of Oltenitza."

Did she imagine it, or was there a hum of surprise?

Then she was moving forward towards the end of the room where the Queen stood waiting. Suddenly she could see everything with brilliant clarity, including the Duke and the ambassador, standing near the throne, their eyes fixed on her.

Slowly, steadily she advanced until she reached the point at which she should curtsey. A presentation curtsey was like no other. It must be very deep, down on one knee to the floor, where it must be held for almost a minute.

Then, rise and advance. Other debutantes kissed the Queen's hands, but as 'royalty' Ola was exempt. Instead Victoria leaned towards her and kissed her forehead.

She was smiling, very slightly, and her lips moved to murmur, "Well done."

Now the most difficult part. She rose and stepped back, reached behind her and gathered up her train. Slowly she retreated along the crimson carpet, until the doors swallowed her up again.

At last she could let out her breath in relief.

"You did splendidly," said the kindly Lady Cadwick.

Before Ola could leave, the ambassador came to find her and thank her again.

"My gratitude," he said. "You were very convincing, and there were several people there who were astonished."

"I hope I may have done some good," she said. "Is

there any news from your country?"

He shook his head sadly.

"I look forward to seeing you again tomorrow," he said.

"Tomorrow?" Ola asked, puzzled.

"Tomorrow night there's a dinner in Buckingham Palace for visiting royalty and ambassadors," the Duke explained. "Afterwards there is a ball."

"Your presence at both will be very helpful," the ambassador said. "My friend here, the Duke of Camborne, will escort you. So you will be all right. He will take good care of you."

"Yes," said Ola in a colourless voice. "I know he will take care of me."

The Duke drew her aside.

"Return to your hotel," he said, "and have something to eat. This afternoon I shall take you out for a drive in the carriage. It's important that you should be seen in public. Please be ready at three o'clock."

"What about Greta? Surely my lady-in-waiting should accompany me."

"I hardly think – "

"She doesn't like being left alone in the hotel. After what happened last time, she's frightened."

"But surely she's not alone there now?"

"No, one of Lady Cadwick's maids is with her. I should much prefer that she comes too."

He looked at her sadly for a moment.

"There's no need for this, Ola."

"What did you call me?"

"I meant, of course, Your Royal Highness. It is quite unnecessary to take Greta with us."

"I wish her to come," Ola said firmly.

101

He gave a small bow.

"As Your Royal Highness pleases."

'It doesn't please me,' she thought. 'It breaks my heart. But what else can there be between us now?'

Lady Cadwick took her away for the journey back to the hotel. There she stood in the centre of her room while they all helped her to disrobe.

The ostrich feathers were removed, then the diamond tiara, then the magnificent gown, bearing the Grand Order of Oltenitza, First Class.

Gradually 'Princess Ola' was vanishing, leaving behind only herself. And she was no longer quite certain who she was.

Lady Cadwick removed the order and handed it to Greta.

"Princess Ola must wear this at the banquet and ball tomorrow night," she said.

Greta nodded and put the decoration away carefully.

When they were alone, Ola told her about the arrangements for the rest of the day, and Greta smiled.

"We will be all right now the Duke has taken charge," she said.

"Greta, we have to stop thinking of him as a friend. All the time I thought he was – " her voice shook, but she forced herself to recover, "all that time, he was going back to this terrible man to report everything we said or did."

"But you cannot blame him for that," Greta pointed out reasonably. "If he realised right from the start that you were an impostor, what was he supposed to do?"

"I don't know. It's just that when I think of the things he said to me, and I said to him – "

"You never really told me what happened that first night you went out with him," Greta observed hopefully.

Ola sighed.

"It doesn't matter now. It's over and done with. Let's plan what we're going to wear this afternoon."

"I'm really going too? Wouldn't you and he rather be together?"

"And leave you alone here, trembling every time there was a knock on the door? You were distinctly nervous, I recall."

"Yes, but not now. Nothing will happen while we're under the Duke's protection. I know you're not friends with him any more, but he has to keep us safe or be in trouble with the Queen. I'm happy to stay here so that you two can talk and sort it out."

"I'm a Princess," Ola said. "I don't go out without my lady-in-waiting."

As she spoke an expression of stubbornness settled on her face that Greta had never seen before. It was as though Ola had become somebody else.

At three o'clock precisely the Duke was waiting for them below. He bowed to Ola and greeted Greta graciously. Although he had not wanted her to come, his good nature prevented him from revealing this in his manner.

Also, he was beginning to feel that, since Ola was clearly not going to soften towards him, a third person might be useful.

As they drove towards Hyde Park he said,

"The two of you have a great deal to learn before tomorrow night. You must know about Oltenitza, as it will be fatal if anyone catches you out. You should, for instance, know about the port of Rizena, on the Aegean Sea, through which much of the county's prosperity comes."

"You mean, it isn't land locked?" asked Ola, recalling her own blunder with a wry smile.

"No, Your Royal Highness. In fact, I suggest that you

travelled from that port."

"Oh yes," she agreed. "I remember telling you so."

"Indeed you did. I believe you also mentioned that your brother Piers and your sister Ludmilla came to see you off, before returning to their home in Hollentot Castle."

And she had claimed to be an only child.

Although the Duke had told Ola that he had seen through her from the start, it was only at this moment that it became real to her.

She had been so sure that she could treat this as a game, with no idea of the powerful forces ranged against her. So she had blundered and blundered, and now she felt incredibly foolish.

She had blamed John for betraying her to Danson, but the truth was a thousand times worse.

How he must have laughed at her!

While she had been losing her heart to a man who seemed charming and warm-hearted, he had actually been enjoying the joke against her.

She felt she could bear anything but his derision.

She closed her eyes against the pain that swept over her. Now she opened them again and faced him with cool dignity. It was the only way she could bear it.

"Naturally they came to see me off," she said. "After which, they returned to the Castle, and were then trapped there by the Russians, where they have been ever since."

"How do you know this?" he said quickly. "It happened after you left."

"You told me," she replied. "When I arrived here, you informed me of the misfortune that had befallen my country."

"And advised you to remain here where you are safe, rather than yielding to your understandable desire to return home and help your family and your countrymen," he supplied.

"Yes, that was it. I realised that my best course was to stay here and seek the help of Her Majesty."

"Well done."

"But wait. How did you know about my family's fate."

"There are agents in the field who send back information to appropriate sources."

"Ah yes!" she said with an air of remembering. "Sir Bernard Danson is so excellent at his job, is he not? So accurate."

"Sir Bernard is an ambitious man," the Duke said through gritted teeth. "It sometimes leads him to jump to conclusions."

"But of course he can only act on the information presented to him," Ola pointed out sweetly. "And so much must depend on the way it is presented."

After a sulphurous silence the Duke asked,

"May I enquire if Your Royal Highness meant anything particular by that remark?"

The 'Princess' regarded him with an imperious eye.

"Let us merely say that he is probably not the only man who may sometimes exaggerate," she told him.

After that, not another word was said until he returned Ola and Greta to the hotel, and informed them, in a colourless voice, that he would call for them both at seven.

"I have a special treat for you tonight, for I'm taking you to the theatre," he explained. "Lady Krasler, do you manage to see theatrical performances very often?"

"I have never seen one," said Greta in a thrilled voice.

"Then I shall look forward to your enjoyment. Good day, Your Royal Highness."

Ola climbed the stairs seething. She had half formed the intention of taking Greta at her word and going without her that evening.

Now the Duke had made that impossible, and it crossed her mind that he had done it on purpose.

Now it was *he* who did not want to be alone with *her.*

*

Greta was so delighted at her first visit to the theatre that Ola was determined not to spoil it for her, and did her best to enter into the spirit of the occasion.

They helped to dress each other, for now Greta could wear one of the silk dresses Ola had bought her on the first day.

Ola's own gown was a very pale yellow silk, which threw her auburn hair into dramatic relief. But choosing jewels for it was a problem.

Her mother's jewels were of good quality, and had seemed suitable until then. But the diamond tiara she had borrowed from Lady Cadwick had been on a different level entirely. That, Ola now realised, was how royalty should dress, and she could not do so.

"I can't wear pearls with this colour," she said. "I need something warm."

"There are your garnets," Greta said, sounding doubtful. Garnets could never compete with diamonds.

Ola made a face.

"Yes. My garnets. Oh dear."

There was a knock on the outer door. Greta went to answer it and Ola heard the Duke's voice. She hastened out of her room.

He was splendid in white tie and tails, a crimson satin lined opera cloak over his shoulders.

He bowed.

"Forgive me for coming early Your Royal Highness," he said, "but I wanted you to look at these. I believe they would be suitable for you to wear."

He was carrying a black velvet box, such as was usually used to carry jewels, except that this was larger than usual. Before their astonished eyes he opened it out onto the table.

Both women gasped.

Inside was the most fabulous set of emeralds and diamonds that they had ever seen.

There was a tiara, a heavy, two strand necklace, earrings, a bracelet, a ring. They were more than merely beautiful and expensive. They were luxurious, fabulous, exotic, glorious.

They were jewels for a Princess.

"I guessed well," the Duke remarked. "They will be perfect with that gown."

"But – where do they come from?" Ola breathed.

"They belong to my family."

"Then I can't wear them," she said at once. "They must be well known and will be recognised."

"Not at all. My mother wore them once thirty years ago. Since then no other woman has worn them. They were lodged in the bank's vaults, where they have remained ever since. I promise you, nobody will know them."

The emeralds and diamonds gleamed and glistened like stars, tempting her.

"It is essential that you wear them," the Duke said firmly.

While she still hesitated, he lifted the necklace and went to stand behind her. He was eight inches taller than Ola and it was easy for him to drape it around her neck. She felt his fingers lightly touching her, then the jewels cold against her skin.

He stepped back to allow Greta to fit on the ear-rings, then the tiara and the bracelet.

A truly magnificent woman looked back at Ola from the mirror.

Slowly she rose and began to move about the room, trying to accustom herself to the weight of the jewellery. When she felt a little more confident she turned.

The Duke was regarding her with a look in his eyes that she did not understand. He seemed thunderstruck.

"Not every woman can wear magnificent jewels," he said. "But you do them justice."

"You think they will help me play my part convincingly?" Ola asked.

He seemed to come out of a dream.

"Your part – yes, indeed. You will play your part perfectly, I know. Now ladies, shall we be on our way?"

CHAPTER EIGHT

On the journey the Duke told them they were going to the Savoy Theatre, to see a performance of *Princess Ida* by Gilbert & Sullivan.

"It's an operetta," he explained, "about a Princess who decides she doesn't want to marry, so she founds a university of like-minded ladies, and withdraws from the world."

"What's the point of that?" demanded Greta, scandalised.

The Duke grinned.

"It makes the Prince chase after her, and fight to win her hand."

"That's all right, then," said Greta, sounding satisfied. "It doesn't do to give the gentlemen too easy a time."

The Duke gave Ola a wry look.

"I know somebody who agrees with you," he said.

The 'Princess' loftily disdained to answer this, looking out of the carriage at the street, where she was attracting much attention. People gaped at her glittering jewels and her regal manner.

She was getting into the way of it now, and could adopt a majestic air. So she sat there, looking royal, wondering if the Duke thought her beautiful, and castigating herself for caring.

It was only a short journey to the Savoy Theatre and soon she was being handed down the carriage steps to sweep into the theatre, her hand lightly on the Duke's arm, with 'Lady Krasler' bringing up the rear in stately fashion.

It occurred to her that Greta was enjoying all this. She would have enjoyed it herself if her heart had not been aching.

The manager of the theatre bowed before 'Princess Ola' who inclined her head graciously.

"The Royal box is ready for Your Royal Highness."

The box was large and elegant, with chairs of gilt and plush. In deference to the rule that royalty arrives last, the rest of the audience were already present, and as the box protruded into the auditorium they all had a clear view of Her Royal Highness advancing to the front.

What they did not see was the Duke of Camborne gently taking hold of her elbow to prevent her from sitting too soon, or hear his murmur of,

"Keep standing while they play your national anthem."

She remained still, her head high on her long neck, while the orchestra played 'her' national anthem. The Savoy Theatre was famed as the first public building in London to use electric light, and now that light winked and sparkled off the Camborne diamonds and emeralds.

Down below the crowd 'oohed' and 'aahed' at the beauty of a Princess who looked exactly how a Princess ought to look. And when the music finished they applauded her.

She smiled and acknowledged the tribute. Then the Duke drew out a chair for her to sit, took his place beside her, and the lights went down.

Afterwards she could never remember any details of the performance. All she was aware of was the Duke, sitting close. She could hear his voice when he laughed, and sometimes she thought he was looking at her, not the operetta.

The force of his look made her tremble, and she longed to speak to him, to find the words that would end their quarrel.

But there were no such words.

She could never blot out the memory of his kiss, and her own passionate response to it, and all the while he had been reporting back to British Intelligence.

One part of her she knew she was being unreasonable. After all, it was she who had started everything and as Greta had said, what else could he have done?

But this had nothing to do with reason. This was a matter for the heart. And her heart felt betrayed and disillusioned.

After the performance he took them both to dine in a fashionable restaurant, where once again Ola received stares and admiration.

"You would think they had never seen royalty before," she observed.

"Yes, but you look like royalty, and many of the real ones don't," said the Duke with a grin.

She noticed that he spoke with perfect composure, and seemed not in the least troubled by the coolness between them.

Perhaps he did not care.

Perhaps it even suited him.

When their food had been served he spoke in a businesslike fashion.

"We need to settle the details for tomorrow. It's the great day of the celebrations, the day when Her Majesty rides in state to Westminster Abbey for the service of Thanksgiving. I shall be on duty and unable to be with you, so I wish you both to remain at the hotel."

"Certainly," said Greta obediently.

"There is no certainly about it," Ola said at once. "Perhaps I should like to go out and watch the procession to the Abbey."

"No," said the Duke at once.

"In other words, I'm still under suspicion," Ola flashed.

"My dear," Greta protested. "The Duke knows best. He's only thinking of your welfare."

"No, he's thinking I might assassinate the Queen on her journey. Don't be fooled by all this, Greta. He still doesn't trust me."

The Duke stared at her and for the first time that evening the mask fell from his face, leaving behind pure, raging anger.

"*Don't be ridiculous!*" he said with soft vehemence.

She stared at him, shocked by the blazing fury in his eyes. For the first time she realised that this was a man at the end of his tether. Some violent, suppressed emotion was driving him on, even while he played the smooth courtier.

He calmed down. The courtier's mask was in place again.

"You misunderstand me," he said. "As Lady Krasler says, I am concerned for your welfare. You have attracted a lot of attention, and if you go out without me tomorrow, I'm concerned that some situation may arise that you would be unable to deal with.

"Suppose, for instance, that somebody confronted you, speaking Oltenitzan? It would be no use saying that you only spoke German."

"I suppose I got that wrong too?" she said crossly.

"No, you got that right. German *is* the aristocratic

112

language of Oltenitza. I congratulate you. But if someone is intent on discovering the truth about you, he would certainly test your knowledge of the local language. Without me there to intervene, you could easily be in difficulties.

"So please oblige me by taking no risks, and agreeing to remain in your hotel suite."

"We shall do so," Greta said at once.

Ola glared indignantly, but she could not defy the Duke now, after the astounding look she had seen in his eyes.

"You can spend the day studying some books that I shall leave with you tonight," the Duke continued. "They will tell you about 'your' country, so that you can appear knowledgeable at the banquet tomorrow night.

"I appreciate that you would rather be out enjoying yourself with the crowd, but you are now working for British Intelligence, and we all have to obey our orders."

"Indeed we do," she said, giving him a level gaze. "Orders must be obeyed, whatever the cost."

Their eyes met. His own were suddenly full of sadness.

"Whatever the cost," he agreed quietly.

After that the evening died. Conversation was spasmodic, and they were all relieved when it was time to return to the hotel.

The Duke handed the books to Greta and saw them to the door.

"Until tomorrow evening," he said. "I shall call for you at six o'clock. Goodnight, Your Royal Highness."

Although there was nobody to see them here, he bowed formally. Then he took his leave without a backward glance.

*

113

"I don't know how we're going to get through all these," Greta said next morning, spreading out the books on the table. "But if we work hard we should become familiar with the map and the principle cities."

"I hope you do," said Ola, pinning a hat onto her head. "You can tell me all about it when I return."

"My dear, whatever are you doing?"

"I'm going out. Did he really think I was going to be cooped up in here all day with everyone else watching the procession?"

"But you said – he said – "

"He said I had to obey orders. *His* orders! Oh no!"

She headed for the door but Greta got there first and stood before it with her arms folded.

"Greta, I'm warning you – "

"Oho, madam! You're warning me are you? Suddenly you're a Princess! Not with me."

"Greta, please, you simply can't stop me."

"Who said anything about stopping you? I'm coming with you."

Ola gave a crow of laughter.

"There! Now he can't say I'm taking risks."

"You're going to tell him about this?" asked Greta.

"Of course I am. Now hurry up. I don't want to miss the procession."

Feeling like schoolgirls playing truant they slipped out into the street, nearly colliding with a couple of middle-aged women. They were dressed rather mannishly in shirts, ties and straw boaters, and seemed to be giving more attention to the travel guides in their hands than to the street around them.

There were mutual apologies, and then Ola and Greta slipped into the crowds all streaming to the route of the

114

procession. It would travel from Buckingham Palace down the Mall, under Admiralty Arch and then along Whitehall to Westminster Abbey.

In a sudden surge of eagerness, Ola seized Greta's hand and they ran all the way from Piccadilly to the Mall. Terraced benches had been set up along the route, filled with cheering, flag waving people.

It seemed impossible that they could squeeze into one of these packed stands, but someone in the friendly crowd saw them hesitating and yelled, stretching out a hand to them. Somehow they managed to scramble up three tiers.

Now they had an excellent view of the procession, which had already started. To one side it stretched away as far as the eye could see in the direction of the Palace. To the other side it stretched ahead, also as far as the eye could see.

Soldiers everywhere, their different uniforms forming blocks of colour as they rode past. Then came the Indian cavalry, bearing lances as they escorted the Queen's carriage, at her special request. Protected by them, Her Majesty sat in the gilded state landau drawn by six cream horses.

Instead of state robes and crown she wore, as she had insisted, her widow's bonnet. It was as if she wanted the world to see her as a grieving widow, a mother, a grandmother – except that she was grandmother to an Empire.

Ola felt tears prick her eyes as she saw the woman who had trusted her and been so kind to her.

Then the landau had rolled past, to be followed by other carriages bearing the aristocracy, the Dukes, Marquises, Earls, Viscounts, all in their robes of state.

And there was the Duke of Camborne, splendid in a scarlet velvet cloak, with ermine. As his carriage rolled by it seemed to Ola that he looked right in her direction.

Had he seen her in the crowd? Was that a look of

amazement and anger on his face? It was impossible to be certain. But as he moved away she saw him turn his head backwards, as though seeking something he was not certain that he had seen.

And then it was all over, for the moment. The procession passed on to the Abbey, and the crowds were left to enjoy themselves with the numberless entertainments London provided.

There were stalls everywhere. Some sold Jubilee souvenirs, and Greta bought a china mug, while Ola purchased an octagonal plate, both with the Queen's portrait. From another stall they bought two fried sausages and a bottle of lemonade, and then strolled into St. James's park.

There they sat, enjoying the sun and the feeling of having nothing to do but enjoy themselves.

"I'm beginning to understand why royalty likes to get away from being stared at," Ola said with a sigh. "I've only experienced it for a day or two, and already I shall be glad when it ends."

"My goodness, yes!" Greta exclaimed. "You can't even get away from them here. Look at those men staring at you."

Ola followed her finger and saw two men standing near a flower bed. They were watching in a blatant manner, sometimes looking at her, sometimes at each other as though seeking confirmation.

"They've been sent to check my identity," Ola confided in a conspiratorial whisper. "At any moment, one of them will come and speak to me in Oltenitzan."

They chuckled, recalling the Duke's warning.

"What will you do?" Greta asked.

"Nothing. I shall leave that to you. As my lady-in-waiting it's your job to deal with people on my behalf."

"But I don't know Oltenitzan either."

"Then perhaps we'd better leave."

As they walked away Greta said,

"I think I saw them last night as we were leaving the theatre. So they must have seen you there, and they couldn't believe it when they recognised you today."

"Mmm! That must be it."

"Where are we going now?"

"Let's go and stand outside Buckingham Palace. The Queen will be arriving soon."

They managed to get close to the gates just before the crowd began to converge from all directions. After waiting nearly an hour they were rewarded by the sight of the Queen's arrival. A few minutes later she appeared on the balcony and they joined in the cheers.

"And now," said Ola, "I think we should hurry back to the hotel and try to arrive before the Duke descends on me in a fury. Greta?"

Greta did not seem to be listening. She was staring deep into the crowd.

"Greta, what is it?"

"I just thought I saw those two men again, but they vanished."

"How dare he?" Ola said explosively.

"Who?"

"The Duke. I've suddenly understood everything. Those two men work for him. He told them to follow us."

"How could he? He was in the procession."

"He could have sent a servant with a message as soon as he reached the Abbey. We didn't notice them until an hour later, remember? Or he could have arranged for them to wait outside the hotel, to see if we left, and we just didn't notice them. I wouldn't put anything past him. Come on, let's give them the slip."

They hurried away until they had left the crowd behind. Within a few minutes they had secured a cab, and were heading for the hotel, where they enjoyed a good lunch and spent the rest of the afternoon virtuously reading books about Oltenitza, until it was time to dress for the evening.

*

The Duke arrived promptly on the dot of six. And he was in a towering rage.

"Have you taken leave of your senses?" he demanded of Ola.

"Are you talking to me?" she enquired with regal loftiness.

"Don't play your games with me. I saw you in the stands. After I told you – "

"You told me all sorts of absurd things because you didn't want me to see the Queen's procession. Well, I did see it, and you may have noticed that Her Majesty is unharmed."

"Of course she is," he snapped. "It was your safety I was thinking of."

"I, too, am unharmed. The only mysterious followers I saw were yours. And I gave them the slip very easily."

"So it would seem. I must have a word with them." He took a deep breath, as though forcing himself to calm down. "Now let's forget that for the moment. Have you studied your books at all?"

"*Ja, Herr Lehrer!*" she told him brightly.

"What?"

"It means, 'Yes, Mr. Schoolmaster.' I think it suits you."

Greta made the mistake of choking back a giggle. The Duke cast her a fulminating look.

"You know I don't speak German," he snapped.

"But Princess Ola does speak it. Also, Princess Ola

118

does not like being given orders."

"Then Princess Ola is a feather-brained ninny who doesn't know when to listen to wiser heads than her own."

"Princess Ola will be very glad when this is over and she can return to Scotland."

"And some people will be glad to see her go, since she is nothing but trouble," he raged. "Now, are you ready to leave?"

"Quite ready, thank you."

This time Greta was not to travel with them, which Greta, herself, thought was a pity, since this quarrel was shaping up very promisingly. But she would make Ola tell her all about it, when she came home that night. And if the silly girl hadn't been reconciled with the man she clearly loved, then Greta would personally take a hand to make certain that she did.

Tonight Ola's gown was of satin in a colour half way between grey and silver, trimmed with lace. Pink satin ribbons gave it a touch of colour. Tonight she wore her mother's three stranded pearl necklace. In contrast to her gorgeous glitter of the night before, she looked softer.

The Duke took a velvet cloak from Greta and draped it over Ola's shoulders. His anger had died.

"You look very beautiful," he said abruptly.

He sounded awkward, not like the smooth courtier who could cope with every situation, as though something had taken him by surprise.

"Thank you," she said. "You probably think I should be wearing your jewels, but – "

"No, I like you better like this. You are more like yourself. Last night I hardly knew you."

"Last night I was what you made me," she said softly. She too had recovered her temper, and was thinking how handsome he looked.

119

"And tonight?" he asked.

"I don't know."

He gave her his arm and they went downstairs. As his carriage rumbled to Buckingham Palace, she looked up at the evening sky and wondered how much longer this would go on. Where did the road lead, and what lay at the end of it?

At the Palace they were conducted to the Bow Room where the guests were assembling. There had never been such a glittering gathering. Fifty foreign Kings and Princes, all in uniform, were there, along with the Governors of Britain's overseas dominions.

"Who's that huge man with the beard, glaring at me"? Ola asked.

"He's the Russian ambassador. Don't worry. We'll outface him."

And together they did outface him. Try as he might, the ambassador was unable to get close enough to Ola to speak to her.

At last it was time for them to move out of the Bow Room into the Great Dining Room, where they gathered around a table shaped like a horse shoe, with lamps and flowers down the centre.

The Queen entered, wearing a splendid gown embroidered with silver roses, thistles and shamrocks, and escorted by the King of Denmark. She took her place at the head of the table, and the banquet began.

They dined off gold plate, which Ola had heard about in fairy tales, but had not believed existed until now. She felt as though she was moving in a dream. Princess Ola was not real but neither was Ola McNewton. And the man sitting beside her was less real than anything, because soon they would say goodbye. He would vanish, and he would be glad to see her go. He had said so.

She would be left with an empty life.

There were speeches and toasts. She tried to listen but her mind was occupied with the consciousness that the Duke was sitting close to her, his eyes fixed on her, just as in the theatre.

Slowly she turned her head. He was gazing at her with his heart in his eyes, asking her a question.

Was there really no way back?

And then the banquet was over and everyone was rising to move into the Ballroom, where the orchestra was already waiting to play.

A heavily built man with a beard approached them and greeted the Duke as an old friend. This was the Prince of Wales, and he invited Ola to dance.

The Prince was married to one of the most beautiful women in the land, yet he was notoriously unfaithful to Alexandra. Rumours had even reached Ben Torrach, so Ola was not entirely surprised to find that he was looking her over frankly.

"It's such a pity that we shan't have time to get to know each other really well," he said, his charming smile taking the salacious edge off his words.

"Indeed, sir?" Ola was not quite certain how much he knew about her.

"Just heard a rumour, not confirmed yet, but it seems pretty reliable. Hollentot Castle has been relieved. The Russian soldiers have been put to flight."

"In that case – " she said thoughtfully.

"Yes, you'll have to be leaving us when tonight is over. What a shame! Do you know, I think you and I could have been really friendly."

She murmured, "Your Royal Highness is too kind," but she was thinking that nothing on earth could have made her want to be 'friendly' with him in the way he meant.

Her heart belonged to another man, a man she might

121

never see again after tonight.

The Prince of Wales returned her to the Duke, gave her a knowing wink and departed to find a more willing partner.

"I should have warned you about him," the Duke said. "Was he very difficult?"

"Not really, but – " she looked round and dropped her voice, "he told me something."

"Dance with me," he said. "And then nobody else will hear us."

At first they circled the floor in silence. She was thinking that this was the last time, and her heart ached intolerably.

"Tell me," he said.

"This is the end. The Prince told me that the Russian soldiers had been routed outside Hollentot Castle, and the family rescued. He says it's not officially confirmed yet but after tonight – "

"You will have to vanish," he agreed.

"So this is goodbye," she said. "This is our last dance, our last evening."

"Our last kiss?" he asked.

"You can't kiss me here."

To answer her, he dropped his hand and laid his lips on hers. It was over in a moment, too quick to attract attention from the other circling couples.

He searched her face intently.

"Are you really going to say goodbye to me, Ola? Will you go one way, and let me go another?"

Before she could answer he began to move faster, sweeping her away into the music, swirling her too fast to think. She could only hold on to him in bewilderment, and wonder where the dance was taking her.

After all that had happened, could she take the risk of

loving him, and asking him to love her?

She was spinning down a winding road, the end of which she could not see.

CHAPTER NINE

At last they slowed enough to talk.

"Do you still dislike me too much to talk?" he asked.

"I don't dislike you, my Lord – "

"You mustn't say that," he interrupted quickly. "A Princess would call me Camborne, or even John. From you, I prefer John. I remember how sweet my name once sounded on your lips."

"But that was in another life," she whispered.

"But the life we live now will only be brief. Then we have to return to the old one."

"We can't go back to that," she said. "We know too much."

He gave her a wry smile.

"What's really different is that now we each know what the other knows. So we could start being honest with each other at last. Tell me about Ola McNewton. I want to know a lot more about her."

Ola shook her head.

"She isn't very interesting. When we met you thought I was rare and strange, perhaps even a little exotic and exciting."

"Yes, you were that,"

"But Ola McNewton is just a girl who's been nowhere

and done nothing. This is the first time she's even left Scotland."

"Then it will be my pleasure to show her the world. We'll go to Venice and ride in that gondola, and this time neither of us will be alone. And Ola McNewton is a lot more interesting than the Princess, because she's real.

"I know a little about her," he continued. "I know she has so much courage that she isn't daunted by the thought of storming a city and a Palace. That's a woman that I admire.

"I also know that she has a temper that can make a man think twice before he speaks, and make him sorry if he hasn't played by her rules."

He gave her a wry look before adding,

"The trouble is that her rules are a little complicated, and she isn't always fair or reasonable."

"Indeed!"

"Well, I know she prizes honesty, so I thought I'd be completely open and frank." He smiled. "I dare not put Miss McNewton high on a pedestal, because she's so awkward that if I approached her, she'd kick my hat off."

"She doesn't sound very nice," Ola observed.

"I didn't say she wasn't nice. Just awkward, and prickly. And unjust."

"And unreasonable," she reminded him.

"Oh, you know her?" he asked quickly.

"Yes, I know her very well, and I think you should give her a wide berth."

"That would be the sensible thing to do," he agreed. "But she's a very difficult woman to get rid of. I could dismiss her from my life, but how do I dismiss her from my mind and heart?"

"Very easily, since you've never met her," Ola reminded him.

"Yes, and yet I feel I've known her since the beginning of time."

"Forget her," said Ola. "You and she could never live in peace."

"You don't think she could ever bring herself to believe me, when I say that I fell in love with her during those two magic days that we spent together?"

"But who did you spend those days with?" she asked urgently. "You didn't know who she was, only who she wasn't."

"You're wrong. I didn't know her name, but I came to know her, and everything I said, was said to her. It was her that I fell in love with. Don't you think she could understand that? It's really very simple."

There was a hint of teasing in the smile Ola gave him.

"You may think it's simple, but she's just awkward enough to make it complicated."

"That sounds like her," he agreed. "But I remember something she said to me on the first night, about each of us wanting to find somebody who would see the worst of us and love us anyway.

"I recall her exact words – 'someone who will understand things we do that might seem strange.' I thought then that only a woman with a great heart could say such a thing, and that she, of all women, would understand about forgiveness."

She looked up at him, stricken. It was true, she had said that. And then she had refused to understand the things he had been forced to do.

Suddenly she saw that there was only one thing she could say to him.

"I love you," she said. "I shall always love you."

His face lost its look of anxiety and broke into radiant joy.

"Ola – my love – my beloved!"

The music was coming to an end. The dance was over, but the world had changed.

The Duke drew in a sharp breath.

"There's the Russian ambassador heading for you again. You mustn't talk to him, at least until we know the truth from Oltenitza. Come!"

He walked firmly from the Ballroom, her hand clasped in his. This was strictly against royal protocol, which decreed that nobody departed before the Queen. But the Duke crossed his fingers and hoped his godmother would understand.

They did not stop running until they reached the ground floor and ran out into the gardens. Here everything was prepared for the great firework display that would finish the evening. This was an occasion for the public as a whole, and they were already beginning to appear.

Marquees dotted the huge gardens. The largest one of all was for the Queen's guests, just behind the canopied dais where Her Majesty would sit to watch the fireworks.

"We have a little time yet," said John, drawing her under the trees and taking her into his arms.

It was as though they kissed for the first time. Now they could begin to understand each other, and find the true love that they had always known must be theirs some day.

He kissed her again and again.

"We might so easily have lost each other," he murmured. "And I could not have borne that. I knew at once that you were the one woman in all the world for me, and I was praying that you would turn out not to be a real Princess, because then how could we have married?"

"Is that what you really want?" she asked.

"I shall not be content until you are my wife. You

belong to me now, and I will never let you go as long as I live."

"That's all I want too," she said happily.

"Ola, I swear I never dreamed that fool Danson would behave so stupidly. I thought he'd see it as an innocent prank, as I did."

"He didn't want to believe me innocent," Ola said with a shudder.

"I think you're right. If he could have caught a real live spy it would have been a triumph for him. He thought his chance had come with you, and he wasn't going to let you go easily.

"But it's over now. After tonight Princess Ola will vanish into thin air, taking her secrets with her and her place will be taken by the Duchess of Camborne."

They embraced again, but for the moment they could have no more time alone. The gardens of Buckingham Palace were rapidly filling up. Lords and ladies, royalty and ambassadors were coming out to take their seats to watch the fireworks.

When they were all in place there was a trumpet fanfare and everyone rose to their feet as the Queen came towards the dais where she was to sit.

She was such a tiny figure in her widow's weeds, the white bonnet on her head, with the white streamers flowing behind. Yet priceless diamonds glittered at her throat, and she looked every inch a Queen and an Empress.

The people watching her cheered from the depths of their hearts. Their voices rang out among the trees. Most of them could not remember a time when she had not been on the throne.

Behind her came some of her family, the Prince of Wales, now appearing as a model husband with his wife and their two eldest sons, Eddy and George, both good looking

128

young men in their twenties.

The Queen acknowledged the cheers then she sat down and listened as the band struck up 'God Save the Queen.' Everyone sang heartily.

Then the audience sat down and waited for the fireworks to begin.

It was such a display, so colourful and brilliant. How high the rockets soared! How gloriously the wheels spun! The crowd oohed and aahed with delight.

Ola had never seen a sight so glorious and spectacular. Eyes shining, she gazed up into the heavens. When she looked down again, she saw John watching her.

"Are you warm enough?" he asked.

"Yes," she said happily. "Being with you keeps me warm."

He did not reply and she saw that he was gazing into the crowd.

"I've just noticed my 'spies'," he said. "They're still on duty, although there hardly seems any point when they lost you so completely this morning."

"Where are they?" Ola was scanning the crowd for the two men she'd seen that day.

"There. Over by that tree."

He raised his hand in greeting, and to her astonishment Ola saw the two women that had been outside her hotel that morning. She and Greta had collided with them, and they had all picked each other up, laughing and apologising.

But surely, she had been followed by two men?

"They are the ones you meant?" she asked, bewildered.

"Yes. Their names are Joan and Mildred, and they're sisters. You'll hardly believe it, but they work for a private detective agency. The man who runs it is an old friend of mine, and he says women are far better than men at ferreting out information, and at following people. Joan and Mildred are actually his aunts and he says they're worth their weight in gold."

"But John – "

"One moment, my dear."

An equerry had approached them, and now said,

"Her Majesty wishes to speak to you, Your Grace."

The Duke bent towards Ola and whispered,

"I won't be long."

He did not wait for Ola to reply but slipped out of his seat and hurried away with the equerry into the darkness.

Left alone, Ola tried to puzzle it out. It had been Mildred and Joan who were watching her, but they had lost her this morning because she and Greta had started to run, and vanished into the crowd.

So who were the two men she had seen?

Then she shrugged.

What did it matter, anyway?

Plainly she was mistaken, and the men she had thought were following her were nothing but a pair of innocent bystanders. When the Duke returned she would tell him, and they would laugh about it together.

If only he would return soon. Now they had confessed their love for each other, she hated being apart from him, even for a moment.

She looked over to where Joan and Mildred were watching her, quizzical smiles on their faces. It would be pleasant to talk to them, she thought, and began to make her way across.

But suddenly a man appeared from the shadows, bowed and said,

"Your Royal Highness."

"Yes?"

"Her Majesty requires you. Please come at once!"

He spoke in what seemed to be a hoarse whisper. For a moment she did not understand what he was saying. Then, as he repeated, "Come at once!" she moved to follow him.

It was dark amongst the trees. The man took her hand and held her arm apparently to guide her or prevent her from falling. As he did so another man she had not noticed appeared on the other side of her.

She supposed this was an extra courtesy because they believed her to be royal. But suddenly she noticed, with a flash of alarm, that they seemed to be moving amongst the trees and not in the direction of the Queen.

Then as she started to say, "I think we are going in the wrong direction," something dark and heavy was thrown over her head.

The next moment she was picked up and carried a short distance. She tried to cry out, but whatever was over her head muffled the sound. Then she felt herself pushed into a carriage. Even as she was thrust down on the seat, they started to move.

She heard the wheels rumbling over what sounded like a road. She could see nothing, and when she tried to struggle she was roughly handled back into her seat. It was then she realised, although it seemed incredible, that she had been kidnapped.

She could not believe it was really happening. Yet when she tried to free her hands, it was impossible to do so. Terrified, she realised that she was being taken away from Buckingham Palace.

She could neither move nor breathe easily. She was completely and utterly helpless.

They seemed to be moving at great speed. She thought they must be out of the Palace grounds and on a more or less empty road. Ola had the horrifying sensation of being carried into nowhere.

It was so hard to breathe that she was afraid she was becoming unconscious. So she tried to keep still and breathe slowly, enough to keep her conscious.

'Please God save me!' she cried inwardly. 'Where am I going? What is happening?'

Although it was difficult to hear clearly, she thought she heard the two men speaking in a language that she did not understand.

Perhaps, it was Russian?

She could only guess, but if they were speaking Russian, then she knew the worst.

The Russians had been baffled by her presence in England, when they thought they had the whole Oltenitzan royal family imprisoned. Clearly the news of the rescue had not reached them, and they had seized her to find out who she really was.

And what would they do when they did find out?

She shuddered.

She was almost unconscious when the carriage came to a standstill and she felt herself being lifted from the seat by the two men. She was still completely covered and unable to move as they carried her from the carriage, then downhill.

Then, by the sudden swaying, she knew that she was on board a ship.

'I'm a prisoner and John will never find me,' she thought frantically. 'If they are taking me to Russia, I'll doubtless be killed or imprisoned as a spy. They will never return me.'

Suddenly they stopped, and she was thrown down on something, perhaps a bunk.

The men were talking again. A third man joined them, speaking loudly, also in the language she thought must be Russian.

'They are taking me away,' she thought in despair, 'and I will never see John again.'

At the thought of him, every nerve in her body seemed to cry out for him to save her.

"Help me! Help me!" she wanted to cry.

But she knew no one would hear her, least of all the Duke.

'Only God can save me now,' she thought.

But it seemed that heaven was far away and perhaps no one, not even God and His angels, would hear her cry for help.

Suddenly the rugs which covered her were pulled off. When she opened her eyes she saw that she really was in a ship, lying on a bed in rather a large cabin. There was only one light and it was a very small one.

The three men were walking out of the room. They did not look back or speak to her but shut the door behind them, and she heard a key being turned in the lock.

For a moment she felt so limp and faint from lack of air that she was unable to move. She shut her eyes and tried to breathe deeply. Slowly she began to feel a little stronger.

'I am right,' she thought, 'they are taking me to Russia. There is no hope for me.'

When the Duke returned he would find the place where she had been sitting was empty and no one would know what had happened to her.

It was then she realised with a feeling of horror that the engines were turning. Soon they would travel down the Thames to the sea, and then to Russia.

'Oh, God,' she thought, 'why did this have to happen to me? Why am I being taken away from everything that I belong to and from the man I love? Will I ever see him again?"

*

The Duke hurried to where the Queen was seated. She was so intent on the fireworks that she did not hear him arrive at her side.

After a moment he bent down and said,

"Your Majesty sent for me and I am here."

She looked up and smiled.

"I want your help badly," she told him.

"What is it ma'am?" the Duke enquired.

"I have just learnt that Prince Victor Paskevich has arrived unexpectedly and uninvited from Russia. I have no wish to talk to him. Please make certain he cannot approach me. He's a drunkard and a boor, and I really can't face listening to any more of his stories about his great-grandfather and Ivan the Terrible."

She was speaking in almost a whisper. The Duke could not help laughing.

"You are quite right, ma'am," he replied, "and I will do my best to keep him away from Your Majesty. Do you happen to know where he is at this moment?"

"Wherever there is strong drink, probably."

The Duke started his search in a huge, decorated tent just behind the royal dais. It was set aside for distinguished visitors, and Prince Victor had no business being there. But, as the Queen had guessed, he had taken up position in the centre of a few other men who had also made an early start on the refreshments.

The Duke did not speak to him because he had a better idea. He knew that once he obeyed the royal command to remain with the Prince, he would never get away from this tedious man.

His salvation came in Teddy and Rick, two brothers in their twenties, whose elder brother had been his friend at school. The Duke had visited their country home, and knew the lads well.

Strictly speaking they, too, should not have been there, but they had gravitated to where the best brandy was to be found.

He went up to them and drawing the elder on one side said, "Teddy, old man, I need your help, and I need it badly. Yours too, Rick."

Teddy regarded him with a look of surprise on his amiable, slightly foolish face.

"What can we do?" he enquired.

"I want both of you to keep Prince Paskevich of Russia from being a nuisance to Her Majesty. That's him over there. Just fill him up with drink. Keep him quiet and keep him occupied."

At that moment a blast of raucous laughter came from Prince Victor, shaking the whole tent.

"Well, keep him occupied, anyway," muttered the Duke.

"Sounds like a good fellow," said Rick, who was deep in his cups.

"Well, he drinks a lot if that's what you mean," the Duke confirmed.

"Prince – what?" Teddy enquired.

"Prince Paskevich."

"Why isn't he with the other royals?"

"He's not royal. In Russia, Prince is just a title, like Duke."

Rick considered this with tipsy gravity.

"Do you mean we don't have to curtsey?" he asked.

"I should strongly advise you against curtseying," said

the Duke. "And you address him as Your Excellency. Oh lord, he's on the move."

The Prince had started making his way out of the tent. The Duke managed to intercept him, saying,

"It is splendid to see you here, Your Excellency, and I do beg of you to come and have a drink with two young men who are very anxious to meet you."

The red faced Prince shook him by the hand.

"A drink is always welcome as you well know," he bawled.

"I do indeed," the Duke replied. "Come to the back of this tent where there is some excellent brandy, which I can thoroughly recommend."

The Prince laughed.

"Then I will certainly sample it. As I am sure the fireworks will go on for hours, there is no reason to hurry."

"No reason at all," the Duke agreed.

He drew him to the back of the tent and introduced him to Teddy and Rick. At once the Prince, delighted to have found a new audience, began to talk very loudly. The more he talked the more they filled his glass, and the more they filled his glass the more he talked.

The Duke heard the words 'Ivan the Terrible', and made a hasty exit, grinning. At last he was free to hurry back to where he had left Ola, and the true start of their life together.

At last all misunderstandings between them were swept away. The future would be what they would make it, one of joy and happiness, where they gave each other nothing but love day after day.

'She is mine and I am hers,' he said to himself, smiling. 'And nothing can part us now.'

CHAPTER TEN

As the Duke made his way back to his beloved Ola, he knew that he was a totally happy man for perhaps the first time in his life.

But when he reached the place where he had left her, to his astonishment he saw that her seat was empty.

'I wonder where she can be?' he thought. 'Perhaps she went to look for me.'

He addressed the elderly lady in the next seat.

"I am sorry to bother you, madam, but I left my friend here a short while ago and now she has disappeared."

The woman smiled.

"Oh, after you had gone an elderly man came up and told her that the Queen wanted to see her."

"Are you sure that was what she was told?" the Duke asked in surprise.

"I am almost certain that was what the man said. But he had a strange accent and was definitely a foreigner, so I might have been mistaken."

The Duke drew in his breath sharply. Suddenly he was full of fear. He knew that Ola had not approached the Queen.

The next moment someone came flying towards him. It was Mildred, one of his 'spies'.

"Your Grace," she said breathlessly, "they've taken her away."

"Who?" he demanded sharply.

"After you left she looked in our direction, and it seemed that she was coming to talk to us."

"I'd just told her who you were," said the Duke.

"And I think she'd recognised us from outside the hotel. Anyway, she was just heading our way when two men pounced on her. They hustled her into a cab before we could stop them. Joan and I ran after them, but they were going at a terrible rate."

The Duke stared at her, full of horror. Who would want to kidnap Ola?

But he knew the answer. It was there in his deepest fears.

The Russians would snatch her to find out how they had been tricked. Prince Paskevich was almost certainly part of the plot. He had not been expected tonight. Nobody had even known that he was in the country, which suggested that he had only just arrived.

He had come straight here in search of Ola, intending to snatch her away and take her thousands of miles away to a wild country.

She was gone, and he might never see her again.

He forced himself to speak calmly but it was very hard through the turmoil inside him.

"Did you notice which direction they took?"

"There was a bicycle leaning against the wall by the gate. Joan took it and went after them as fast she could. She'll be back when she knows more."

"Excellent. Wait here for her. I'll come back."

He started to run back towards the Royal tent. A glance inside told him that Teddy and Rick were still playing their part well, and the Prince was still present, getting drunk.

Then he approached the Queen. As soon as she saw his distraught face she turned to her eldest son, sitting beside her, and said, "Go away, Bertie."

With a grin, the Prince of Wales rose to his feet obediently and vanished.

"What is it John?" the Queen asked. "I can see that something has happened."

Briefly he told her everything, including his fears, and the Queen went pale.

"Get her back," she said at once. "Take whomever you need to help you, but find her. If that brave girl has come to any harm I shall blame myself."

There were several military men present tonight, in glittering dress uniforms, most of them the Duke's friends. He approached two of them, young men with reckless faces whom he knew to be game for any lark.

"Anthony, Jack," he murmured.

It took only a few words to make Major Anthony Hawkins and Captain Jack Estey bid their friends farewell and follow him across the park to where the carriages stood.

The officers went to their own carriages to fetch the pistols they kept under the seats, 'just in case'. They had to leave their weapons there, for they could not have come into the Queen's presence if they were armed.

When they rejoined the Duke he was talking to two middle aged women, one of whom was breathless but doing her best to speak.

"Steady, Joan," the Duke was saying.

"They went along Grosvenor Place and then turned into Birdcage Walk," she gasped. "After that I lost them, they were going so fast."

"Heading for the river," said Jack at once.

139

"It looks like it," said the Duke. "Joan, Mildred, thank you both. Now gentlemen, it's best if you get into my carriage. You won't be seen in there and we can take them by surprise."

The two men climbed in. "Take us to the river, and fast," said the Duke to his coachman.

Fortunately at that time of night the roads were not busy, and they drove towards the embankment at a speed which would have been impossible by day.

Inside the carriage the Duke said, "At this moment Prince Paskevich has no idea we are suspicious of his sudden appearance. That works in our favour, but we haven't much time."

"Are we going to get a good fight out of this?" Major Antony wanted to know.

"A damned good fight," the Duke confirmed.

The two young officers spoke with one voice.

"That's all right then."

At last they reached the embankment, where they could see ships of every sort on the river.

Many people from foreign countries had come to enjoy the Queen's Jubilee and they all seemed to be flying their flag. But for the first half mile or so there was no sign of a Russian one.

Then suddenly the Duke, leaning against the window, saw the Russian ship. He could hear the engines turning, but the ship itself was still.

Fortunately it was close to the side of the embankment and it would be easy to get on to it.

He told his driver to stop and began to walk towards the ship followed by the two soldiers. As they did so, the Duke was praying that Ola was aboard this ship as he believed her to be.

As they stepped on to the gangway, a Russian

appeared who, from his shabby attire, seemed to be a servant.

Sharply the Duke said,

"I wish to speak to the Captain."

As he saw the man had difficulty in understanding what he was saying, he said slowly and emphatically,

"The – Captain – tell him – I am – here– "

Then the Captain himself appeared on deck. He stared at the Duke in surprise, also at the two soldiers behind him, both with pistols in their hands.

The Duke smiled and held out his hand.

"Good evening, Captain," he said. "I am sorry to bother you but on the instructions of Her Majesty the Queen, I have come here to take away a young woman who has been brought aboard by mistake."

"By mistake!" the Captain exclaimed pronouncing the words rather strangely.

At the same time, the Duke was sure he understood what he meant.

"You have been told, or rather Prince Paskevich was told, that the young lady you have aboard is the Princess Ola. That is not true!"

"Not true!" the Captain repeated.

The Duke could see that he was astonished, also a little bewildered.

"She is Scottish," the Duke said, "and as her father was important to Her Majesty, it was a bad mistake to bring her aboard. You could be arrested."

A look of alarm passed over the Captain's face.

"Arrested?" he said slowly.

"Arrested and locked up in the Tower of London," the Duke said emphatically. "You would stay there for ever, and never be heard of again."

He relied on the Captain not knowing that this was impossible. The ploy seemed to be working, for the other man now clearly understood that something was very wrong.

"On Her Majesty's instructions," the Duke continued, "I have come to take the lady away."

The Captain nodded and beckoned the Duke to follow him.

The Duke said to the officers,

"Wait here! But be ready to leave the moment I return."

They nodded without speaking and he followed the Captain below, praying that he had come to the right place.

It seemed to the Duke that the Captain moved rather slowly down to the deck below.

He recognised, when he followed him, that they were now passing the cabins in which, if the ship was carrying anyone of importance, this was where they would sleep.

As they walked further down the passage he realised they were going towards the master cabin.

It was then for a moment he was afraid he was making a mistake.

Surely if the Prince were travelling in this ship he would sleep in the master cabin and the prisoner whatever else they might call her, would be in one of the less important cabins in this corridor?

Unless, he thought, the Prince was planning to join her in the big cabin. The Duke's blood ran cold at the thought of such a threat to his darling.

As the Captain put the key in the lock and opened it, the Duke held his breath.

Ola had been standing by the porthole. As the door opened she turned round. Before the Captain could enter, the Duke moved quickly past him.

When Ola saw him she gave a cry of joy and ran across the room throwing herself against him.

"You've come! You've come!" she said. "I prayed and prayed that you would."

The Duke put his arms round her and held her close against him.

"I have come to take you back," he said quietly, "and there is no need for you to be frightened any more."

Ola gave a sob and hid her face against his shoulder.

Then the Duke said,

"Come at once. We want to get out of this mess before the Prince comes back."

With an effort Ola raised her head from his shoulder. At the same time her eyes were shining as she looked up at him.

"You came for me – " she whispered. "I was afraid you might not understand what was happening."

"I understood," the Duke replied. "But we will talk about it when you are safely in my carriage which is waiting for you."

He turned to the Captain.

"I am sorry, Captain, to have disturbed you, but His Excellency will doubtless be bringing the real Princess aboard when he leaves Her Majesty with whom, at the moment, he is watching the fireworks."

Now the Captain seemed to understand what was happening, and scowled in an unexpected display of stubbornness.

"*Niet!*" he said, barring their way.

But instantly there was a click and a pistol appeared close to his head. The Major was standing there, smiling.

"I know you said to stay up there, old boy," he told the Duke, "but it was devilish dull. I thought it might be more

143

fun down here."

The Captain, eyes bulging with alarm, stepped back and away from the door, leaving room for Ola and the Duke to walk past. The Major came behind them, walking backwards, keeping his pistol trained on the Captain until they were up the stairs.

Jack Estey was there, keeping his gleaming pistol in full view of the crew members who had begun to gather. Major Anthony joined him and the two stood there defiantly while the Duke hurried Ola ashore.

"Thank you, lads," said the Duke fervently.

"You mean that's it?" Jack asked in disgust. "I don't call that a fight."

"I couldn't have done it without you."

The two soldiers grinned and hopped up onto the box with the driver, leaving the Duke and Ola to get into the carriage together.

As they moved away, Ola gave a cry and threw herself against the Duke.

"You saved me," she whispered. "I longed for you, but I didn't dare to hope that you would find me."

Now the tears were running down her cheeks but they were tears of happiness. The Duke put his arms round her and his lips found hers.

As he kissed her, she knew this was what she had prayed for. She felt as if she not only gave him her heart but her soul.

"I love you, my darling, I love you," he said. "Thank God I got there in time."

Then he could no longer speak because he was kissing her again and again.

"I'll never let you go now," he said. "You're mine, whether you like it or not."

"But I do like it," she said. "Oh John, my darling, I thought I would never see you again."

"Do you think I would have let that happen? Don't you know that I would have searched for you to the ends of the earth, even if it took the whole of my life.

"I love you, and I am going to marry you as soon as possible, in case you disappear again. I have never been so frightened in my whole life. If they had managed to get away with you, to Russia – " he shuddered.

Then he was kissing her again.

Kissing her so passionately that Ola wanted to cry from sheer happiness.

"Can we go away somewhere and shut the world out?" she asked him.

"I would like nothing more, my darling, but I'm afraid we must go back and see Her Majesty. She was very concerned about you. And I have unfinished business with Prince Victor Paskevich"

"Who is he?"

"The Russian who sent his men to abduct you. Don't worry, you'll be safe with me, but he has to know that his plot has failed."

"How did you know where to come?"

"Luckily my two spies saw them take you. Joan chased the carriage on a bicycle that she seems to have 'borrowed' from a policeman. She got far enough to tell me your direction."

"I must thank them both. I realise now that I had the clue all the time. The people I saw in the crowd were men. It didn't worry me because I thought you sent them, but they must have been watching me to make sure what I looked like."

"You mean that you never saw Mildred and Joan?"

"I bumped into them outside the hotel, but I didn't

know who they were until you told me tonight. Then I realised something was wrong. I was going to tell you when you came back from the Queen."

The Duke groaned.

"I'll never take my eyes off you again."

When they reached Buckingham Palace, Anthony and Jack rejoined them, the three men walking so that nobody could get near Ola. Together they approached Her Majesty's dais.

Prince Victor was still there, but now he was with the Queen, pouring out an unstoppable stream of words. Strangely, for one who had declared herself bored by this man, Queen Victoria made no attempt to silence him. The few remarks she offered seemed designed to keep him talking, and the Duke realised that his Sovereign and godmother was exerting herself to assist him.

He was sure of it a few moments later when the Prince said,

"I fear I grow tedious. I will leave Your Majesty now."

"Stay where you are," the Queen demanded imperiously. "I am intrigued by your conversation and wish to hear more. You haven't yet told me about Ivan the Terrible."

"But Your Majesty, I have told you all about Ivan the Terrible."

"I forget. Start again."

Trapped, he looked about him, unable to depart in defiance of the royal command, yet eager to be off to the Thames, to take his prize down the river and out to sea, where a Russian warship was waiting.

Just a little longer, he promised himself.

Then his eyes fell on Ola.

He knew it was her, for his agents who had been watching her for days had pointed her out to him when he arrived earlier that evening.

But he couldn't believe his eyes.

He blinked.

Then he swallowed as he realised what this meant.

The Queen had followed his gaze and seen the Duke and Ola standing there. Her face lit up with a smile that was relief as much as pleasure.

"My dear children, there you are! How naughty of you to vanish like that! You've missed such a fascinating talk by Prince Victor Paskevich. Come and meet him."

He was the last man in the world that Ola wanted to meet, but by now she had recovered her nerve enough to look him in the eye and enjoy his dismay.

"Such a pleasure to meet you, Prince," she murmured. "I always felt sure that our paths would cross one day, and now they have. What a pity that our acquaintance couldn't have been longer. Not a pity for me, of course. But a great pity for you."

He understood her. He gobbled like a turkey cock.

The Duke clapped him on the back with dreadful heartiness.

"I'm sure Her Majesty will release you now, old chap, won't you ma'am?"

"Of course. But only with the greatest reluctance," Queen Victoria said, amused.

Her little eyes twinkled. She was enjoying herself.

"So why don't you get off to your ship on the Thames?" the Duke went on. "The Captain wants to have a word with you. And when you get home, empty handed, I dare say the Czar would like a word with you, too."

Prince Victor's face was ghastly. He began to stammer.

"England – a lovely country – I have often thought – I

might – settle here – "

"Goodbye, Prince Victor," said Queen Victoria implacably.

He tottered away.

Smiling, the Queen turned to Ola, who dropped a deep curtsey.

"No, come here, my dear," she said, holding out her arms.

When she had hugged Ola soundly, she said to the Duke,

"Well done, John."

"And thank you, ma'am, for your invaluable assistance in keeping him here," he said, grinning. "It was a noble effort."

"I'm glad you appreciate it. I don't know when I've suffered so much."

"Ivan the Terrible?"

"And the flooding of the Volga," she said with a shudder. "Never mind. I hope never to see him again. Now listen, I have some excellent news. I expect you've heard the rumours from Oltenitza."

"That the royal family has been rescued, ma'am?"

"Yes. It's definite. A group of English soldiers, travelling incognito, did most of the business, but they were helped by the people, who rose against the Russian troops. The whole family is safe, including the Princesses Flaviola and Helola."

"Then it's over?" Ola asked eagerly.

"Yes, my dear. Soon everyone will know that the family is free, and I think you should vanish at once."

"She's going to," said the Duke. "If I may have your permission to leave, ma'am, I would like to take her to Camborne Park, where she will stay until our wedding."

"So I should hope."

"We shall marry quietly, in the little chapel there, and be away from London for some time."

"To give people a chance to forget they saw her in another incarnation," the Queen agreed. "Very wise. Well, I would have liked to attend your wedding in Westminster Abbey, which is where you ought to be married. But I can see that will not be possible.

"When you return to London I shall give a reception for you, and when people see that I accept the Duchess of Camborne, they will forget any passing resemblance to a Princess who is no longer here."

The Duke kissed her hand.

"Dear godmother," he said, "you are too good to me."

"Give me a kiss," the Queen said. "You too, Ola, my dear. And may God bless you both, and make you as happy as I was with dear Albert, but for much, much longer."

*

They stopped at the hotel to collect Greta and the luggage. It was past midnight but nobody wanted to linger. Before dawn broke they were on their way out of London, headed for Hampshire, and Camborne Park.

At first Greta's presence inhibited them, but gradually she nodded off in the corner, and they were able to pretend they were alone.

The Duke took her into his arms and kissed Ola until it was difficult for either of them to breathe.

"You grow lovelier every time I look at you," he whispered. "I'm convinced now that you're not human but someone supernatural, or perhaps an angel who has come from heaven to make me happy."

"All I want to do," she said in a small voice, "is to make you happy, because I'm only happy when I'm with you."

"And I'm only happy when we are together," the Duke replied. "There's no woman in the whole world who is as important to me as you are. If I were offered all the Queens and all the angels, I should not find any of them as wonderful as you."

"I'm just an ordinary girl. Not even a Princess."

"You are Ola. You are my love. There is nothing more wonderful than that."

They kissed again and then she snuggled contentedly against him.

"I'm longing for you to see my home," he said. "I think you'll love it, and the little chapel where we'll marry. The priest will receive you with open arms, because he's always been afraid I would end up marrying someone who loved me only because I was a Duke and not because I was a man."

"You know I love you as a man," Ola answered. "I would love you if you were a crossing-sweeper. I think we've been looking for each other for a long time, although we haven't known it."

"I knew it as soon as I saw you," he replied.

There was silence for a few miles and then she asked,

"Why are you frowning?"

"I was just wondering – why a crossing-sweeper?"

She gave a sleepy, contented laugh.

"It was the furthest thing from a Duke that I could think of. Mind you, I think I prefer you being a Duke, and having all those lovely horses to ride."

"Ah, you're marrying me for my horses?"

"Well, you made them sound marvellous when you talked about them."

"Do you remember all that?" the Duke asked.

"I remember everything you have ever said to me,"

Ola told him. "I want you to remember what I am going to tell you now, because it will never alter. I love you, I love you and there has never been another man in my life and there never will be."

The Duke was very moved.

As he kissed her, he knew he had found what he thought would never be his. A true love that came from the heart, from a woman with a deep, honest soul, who loved him for himself alone, without thought of worldly advantage.

There would never be in either of their lives anyone else of any importance.

A week later, wearing her most beautiful white gown and some of her mother's precious jewellery, Ola was married to the man she loved in the small chapel adjacent to the Duke's great mansion.

The chapel was filled with flowers which scented the air, as the old priest pronounced them man and wife.

"How can it be possible that we are so happy?" the Duke asked later that evening. "How can I have been so fortunate as to find you?"

"My whole heart and soul are yours," she said. "God brought us together and no human being will ever separate us or make us unhappy again."

"Amen to that," the Duke replied.